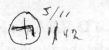

5/11
1/42

Y0-BYV-150

COMES THE REAPER

When youthful immigrant Tom Connor first disembarked at Puget Sound, eager to settle in the northwest with his bride, little did he know that he was to take a long, long journey. It covered the width of the American continent, from Indian uprisings, through the war between the States, and the assassination of a president. This is a saga of violence, death and revenge that bears witness to the emergence of the bounty hunter known to history as The Reaper.

Books by B. J. Holmes
in the Linford Western Library:

DOLLARS FOR THE REAPER
BLOOD ON THE REAPER
THE SHARD BRAND

B. J. HOLMES

COMES THE REAPER

Complete and Unabridged

LINFORD
Leicester

First published in Great Britain in 1995 by
Robert Hale Limited
London

First Linford Edition
published 1998
by arrangement with
Robert Hale Limited
London

British Library CIP Data

Holmes, B. J.
    Comes the reaper.—Large print ed.—
Linford western library
    1. Western stories
    2. Large type books
    I. Title
    823.9′14 [F]

    ISBN 0–7089–5283–6

Published by
F. A. Thorpe (Publishing) Ltd.
Anstey, Leicestershire
Set by Words & Graphics Ltd.
Anstey, Leicestershire
Printed and bound in Great Britain by
T. J. International Ltd., Padstow, Cornwall

This book is printed on acid-free paper

For Sam

Foreword

THE long-lasting absence of law along the western frontier of the United States during the latter half of the last century led to the phenomenon known to history as 'the bounty-hunter'. Unfortunately for students of the period, no systematic contemporary record was kept of the payment from public funds made to private citizens for delivery to the authorities of wanted persons. Therefore, as the evidence of their very existence is anecdotal, compounded by myth and legend, there can be no quantitative comparisons, no grisly league tables.

However, study of a particularly valuable cache of historical documents now lodged in the Archive Department of the Calpone Foundation Library has shown the name of one recipient of bounty payments to appear with noticeable regularity during the period. Nothing is known about him apart from his name, Jonathan Grimm, and that records show his fading signature on receipts for twenty-six men brought in dead or alive. With the data being incomplete, the actual figure that could be credited to him is likely to be even greater. Irrespective, the statistic as it stands must put him near the top of the league table of those men who earned their living by this questionable means.

Some speculative episodes in Grimm's later life have already been chronicled — see *Guns of the Reaper, Dollars for the Reaper, Blood on the Reaper* and *A Coffin for the Reaper* (published by Robert Hale). But from whence did the man come? And what set him on the bounty-hunting trail? The following text pieces together his possible beginnings . . .

1

"CAN'T we settle here, Tom?"

Two figures were standing on the shoreline. The settlement behind them had been known as Dwampish until the white man had recently renamed it Seattle. Timbered houses straggled from the shoreline of the bay village to the forest. From their vantage point the couple could see the evening glory of the Olympic Mountains across Puget Sound.

"It looks so beautiful," she murmured.

Tom Connor pulled his wife close. "Aye, lass, it's got charm right enough. But, Kate, it's deceiving. This place is going to grow rapidly. The trickle of settlers coming in is going to become a tide. It won't be so pretty in five years' time. The place will be busting with people."

"What's wrong with being among

3

people anyway?" She was tired of travelling.

"Nothing, lass. But we want room to expand and grow, don't we? Room for our kids to breathe and run. That's why we came west. And what's more, because there are people here already you just can't settle anywhere. All the land hereabouts is spoke for. You gotta buy it if you want it. And it's so damned expensive. We've only got enough cash left to buy ourselves a wagon and provisions. It would take me years working here to save enough to buy just a little piece of soil to call our own."

It had been a costly and exhausting passage for them. Two months ago they'd started out from Boston by ship. What was intended as a three-day crossing of the Isthmus had become three weeks in an expensive Panama hotel when Kate had gone down with some unidentified illness common to the region. Then up to San Franscisco by steamer and from there a long trip

4

to Fort Vancouver.

"Now treaties are being signed by the Indians," he went on, "the place is going to become more attractive and things are going to get congested round here. But land's still free for the taking further west. We got to grab ourselves a piece while we still have the chance."

Time was running out for the Connors. They'd married in their thirties and Kate's first child had been stillborn. For them, with all their savings gone, it was a last chance.

She snuggled into him to protect herself from the chill wind coming across the Sound. "What you say is true, Tom, but the problems we talked about before we set out are getting bigger in my mind."

"What problems?" he said reassuringly. Kate had always been a worrier.

"Like getting across the mountains. Doesn't seem such a feasible idea now we're here and we can see the size of the mountains."

"Listen. The facts of the situation

were in the newspapers back East. And they're confirmed by discussions I been having with folks here since we arrived. There are several passages across the Cascade Mountains. Why, two summers ago one group even crossed the range with a huge herd of cattle. Dunna fret, lass, the trail's a well-worn one now. And the wagons they make here are small ones, especially made for the local conditions. Not like those heavy prairie schooners you seen pictures of."

They'd heard the buzz saws in the timber mills singing all day.

She paused. Then, "And Indians. What about Indians? I heard some horrible things on the boat."

"You shouldn't listen to tittle-tattle," he reprimanded. "Washington Territory has got a new governor — Governor Stevens — and his first job is to make treaties with all the Indians under his jurisdiction. They're all signing. The Nisquali, the Puyallup, the Yakima. All of them. Do you know, he's crossed the whole damn territory — that's nearly a thousand miles. Making friends with redskins all the way. It was in the paper today. He's reached Nebraska and has got the Blackfeet to sign. No, the redmen aren't hostile. They're as eager to keep peace as the white man. They're getting land called reservations, and lots of supplies as part of the treaties: seeds, corn, tools for farming. They're even going to get money every year from the government."

"Well, Thomas Jonathan Connor," she said. "I wish I had your confidence. That's all I can say."

He chuckled dismissively and tightened his grip around her shoulders. "Come on, lassie. Let's get between those warm sheets."

They turned and walked toward the twinkling lights of the seafront shack that constituted the hotel. But deep down Tom wasn't as confident as he sounded. His worries were mounting too. He was increasingly concerned, not about Indians or the capability of wagons crossing mountain ranges. He was secretly concerned about the weather. Because of Kate's illness en route, they'd arrived at Seattle much later than he had planned. He'd spoken with old-timers in the saloon that evening and they had assured him that the weather would hold for another month. But he didn't like the wind now scything like an icy blade across the Sound.

* * *

Six wagons slithered in an ungainly pattern down the mountain trail. Four were occupied by miners and their equipment. A fifth contained provisions for the settlement at Walla Walla. The Connors were last in line and were the only settlers in the train. The couple had thoughtfully timed their journey for the warmer months but, because of the unscheduled delay, they were still travelling as winter approached. Tom had ignored his suspicions about the weather but his unease had been well-founded. The relentless wind blustering across the Canadian border was fast getting colder.

Thankfully the first snow had been delicate and had come after the small procession had made the ascent of the final incline in the journey. They were now less than a day's journey from the small settlement at Walla Walla, their destination. There had been problems during the two weeks trek. On many occasions ascents could only be made one wagon at a time with wooden spars levered under back axles and with many shoulders heaving at the rear. Descents were nearly as bad. Even now, like other men, Tom was staggering alongside his faltering wagon, locking the rear wheels with his wooden spar. Braking in this way was effective in reducing the speed but it made the wagon more difficult to steer. Kate, in her fight with the reins to restrain the horses, had lurched awkwardly sidewards across the seat as the wagon slewed downwards at an angle.

Tom was glad to see her managing. If his delicate Scottish rose could handle horses and wagon under these conditions, she had the makings to cope with farming life on a settlement.

"We'll rest here a piece," came the shout from the lead wagon as it reached a rare level part of the rough mountain trail. One by one the wagons levelled and came to a standstill

Tom leant against the wagon side, breathing heavily, his eyes closed. His eyelids fluttered as he grabbed for air, then, regaining his breath he opened his eyes fully and looked about him. He observed how the resting party were dwarfed by their surroundings. It was truly a land of giants. Not only were the mountains on a grander scale than was ever imagined by the Scotsman but even the trees were enormous. His eyes moved up the slope taking in the towering Sitka spruce and massive Douglas fir. It was then he saw movement. Figures coming down the snowy incline, flitting like ghosts amongst red alder.

"Hey," he shouted to the leader of the train, a gnarled old miner by the name of Seth who was checking the wheel rim of his wagon. "Look yonder. We got visitors."

Seth looked in the direction Tom was pointing, screwing up his old eyes against the glare of snow.

"Look like Yakima to me," the oldster concluded after he'd made a study.

"They're friendly, ain't they?" Tom shouted.

"Should be," Seth replied. "But don't look it to me. They're usually quite open in approaching whities. Don't usually come a-sneaking up like that."

He pulled himself up on to the hub of a wheel in order to better address the column. "Be prepared, folks. There's supposed to be treaties with these redskins but put slugs in the breech — just in case."

Tom nervously checked his Walker Colt, purchased on the advice of veterans back in Seattle, and pushed it into Kate's hand after she'd shuffled down from the buckboard seat with skirts gathered. His rifle levered and ready he waited with his wife behind their wagon like the other travellers.

Now there was nothing to see. The ominous progression of redmen down the slopes had apparently stopped.

"Get ready," Seth shouted in a crackly voice as wizened as his face. "They ain't approaching us open. The varmints are up to something."

"Thought they were supposed to be friendly," Tom shouted, turning his eyes momentarily from his rifle sight. "Signed treaties and things."

"Treaties or no treaties," one of the miners rejoined, "out here anything goes. And them critters don't look like they's a-coming down here to discuss philosophy."

Tom and Kate exchanged glances and then looked back up the slopes.

The wind fell to a breeze, working the powdery snow to soften the contours of the terrain. Above its gentle swish nothing was heard during a long interval except for the beating of wings as a flock of trumpeter swans scudded southward.

Then they came. God knows how many. Every tree seemed to produce its own screaming apparition. Down the slope they came, some slithering, others leaping through drifts, billows of snow spraying from their legs. The forerunners dropped into the snow, almost out of sight, and began firing from prone positions. A mixture of bullets and arrows peppered the wagons.

Tom was scared, more than he'd ever been in his life. But he told himself not to panic. He had to set an example for Kate. He lined his sights on an Indian who had leapt out from the cover of a tree and was running faster than the others down a rare stretch of hard ground. Encased in furs the attacker presented a sizeable target. Tom squeezed the trigger and the man spun sideways as the bullet ripped into his body.

Other Indians fell — but some were getting through. Damn, his gun jammed. It was probably something simple to correct but he didn't have time for lengthy investigations. He turned to take Kate's weapon but she was already clicking on an empty chamber. He had no time to reload. Several redmen were almost upon them. He grabbed the wooden spar that he had cursed so much when it had blistered his hands yet had been indispensable in manoeuvring their wagon up and down the mountain trails.

One Indian wielding an axe was thundering to the edge of the small bluff to the fore of the Connors' wagon. Such was the man's impetus that he clearly intended leaping across to the buckboard. He had seen the trouble the Connors were having with their firearms and was prepared to fight at close quarters.

Tom circled the wagon and waited just below the overhang, gripping the heavy spar so that it was vertical, its end resting on the ground. From his low position he couldn't see their attacker but he soon heard the man's feet pounding the hard ground above him. He heaved the spar upward and forward just as the Indian launched himself across the void. With hands raised, the man's arms presented no protection for his face which, together with his chest, took the impact of the upward-moving beam. There was a sickening sound as the redman buckled in mid-air and fell backward to the ground. Tom grunted as the force of the violent connection travelled along his arms. He looked down at the smashed face of the man drunkenly working his elbows in an attempt to get to his feet in a world which had suddenly become confusing. Instinctively Tom raised the beam and brought it down on the Yakima's head.

Something cracked. He looked on the bloody mayhem he had wrought and confirmed the man was no longer a threat.

By now the general noise of the mêlée was spooking the horses along the line and one by one wagons began moving crazily as terrified animals reared and strained at their loads.

"Get on the wagon!" he shouted to his wife. "We have no choice."

He pushed her up to the seat and released the brake. The buckboard shot forward but the preceding wagon had got jammed into the bluff. In a frenzy the Connors' horses tried to get around the blockage but there was not enough space on the mountain trail.

As the right-hand wheels began to slither over the edge of the drop he pushed Kate clear but the wagon angled too fast for him to make it. The last thing Tom remembered was the ear-shattering neighings of his horses being dragged over the edge.

2

ALL was quiet when he opened his eyes. His body was cold, bruised, aching. But it was the quiet that registered: that meant the fighting was over. He looked about him. His partially cushioned descent had been around a hundred feet and he had come to rest in some bushes.

Christ, Kate, he thought, getting unsteadily to his feet. He could see where he'd landed and the channel through the snow where he'd rolled. The fact that he'd fallen unimpeded for some of the distance, and thus leaving no immediate trail in the snow, explained why no Indians had come down to investigate him. He would have been finished off for sure. Far below he could see the wagon and the grotesque, inert shapes of bloodied horses.

He climbed unevenly back to the trail. There was not a soul left living. With redness stark against the snow, crimson stains pinpointed where fallen defenders had been butchered. Near to puking and afraid of what he would find he investigated each mutilated corpse. He didn't know whether it was good or bad that he found no Kate.

Everything usable had been taken from the bodies and wagons. His teeth chattering he examined the corpses in turn once again, then explored the perimeter of the scene but found no single tracks. Kate was not here, nor had left the place alone. There was a flattened road of snow back up the mountain where the victorious raiders had made their way. All he could think of was — the savages had his wife. And he could plainly see where they had gone. He knew Walla Walla was not far away. Not the odds, not the cold, not the harsh terrain, nothing registered save one thing: he would get help and guns and fetch his Kate back!

18

* * *

Three hours later he reached Walla Walla. It was a disappointment. A few shacks clustered around the rough trail. Small though the place was, it was a hive of activity as people around the town were loading up wagons. He almost collapsed with exhaustion outside the first house.

"Dearie me," an ageing lady said as she opened the door. "What's the matter?"

"Indians," he managed to say. "I was with a small wagon train out of Seattle. Attacked by Indians. They got my wife."

The woman bit the back of her hand as her husband came to the door. "Injuns?" the man echoed. The word was delivered loud enough to register amongst the advancing onlookers, already curious at the sight of the man who had stumbled into their town.

Tom was helped inside by the husband to stand gratefully at the fireside. As he recounted his story the group crowding into the small room grew, the matter being of communal interest.

"That confirms it," one said when Tom had finished. "That's the third attack. The first one might have been an isolated incident like some folks would have us believe. But it's obvious there's a big uprising on."

Listening to the ensuing conversations, Tom realized that some of the settlers had already decided to leave. That explained the wagons being loaded that he had seen on his arrival. But the way people were now talking and moving out of the room it looked like his story was prompting the remainder to join the exodus.

"What about my wife?" he said in a weak, pitiful voice. His query was met by silence. One by one his audience left. They'd heard enough and had their own affairs to think of.

"I gotta get her back," he continued. "What's gonna happen to her?"

"It's probably already happened," one plain-speaker said bluntly. "You gotta face reality. I know it's difficult but the best for you is to forget about it — and concentrate on saving your own skin. The way this looks it ain't gonna be long before they come down here a-hooting and a-hollering and scalping anything that moves."

Tom breathed deeply. It was plain there was no chance of his getting help here. His return to the mountains, for that was the only thought in his head, would have to be a one-man job. But he was enough of a realist to know that his body was no use to him in its present condition; food and sleep were first.

★ ★ ★

When he awoke next morning the settlement was already over half empty. He could see wagons at staggered intervals along the trail in the direction of Spokane. He went to the general store where the owner would be the last one to leave having three wagons to load.

"Is everyone running?" Tom challenged in frustration as he watched the man stripping his shelves.

"You're damn right we are," the storeman said without breaking from his task. "We're all getting the hell out of here. The Yakima have lighted the fuse and we're sitting on the powder keg." He went to the window, pulled back the curtain and peered up the snow-covered slopes. "They'll be down here next — whooping and a-hollering, killing and looting. Eventually the government will send troops. But they'll be too late to save this place. Whatever happens, it's gonna be one helluva bloodbath."

"You don't understand. They've got my wife, my Kate. I can't just do nothing. I've got to get to them, get to their camp. Maybe the redskins will listen to me. Maybe I can strike some kind of bargain."

The man laughed a humourless, sardonic laugh. "Listen, lad. Whatever the varmints have done to your wife, you don't wanna know. And if you go traipsing up there you'll find out to your cost they ain't interested in no bargains." The man returned to his task, scuttling about the store gathering items.

Tom rubbed his forehead. He often got head pains when he was in a tight spot. "Judas Priest. I gotta do something."

"You're crazy. You've said yourself you ain't from these parts — so you don't know the region. The winter looks as though it's setting in early. You can die up there of cold in half a day if the weather takes a bad turn. And it's plain the Yakima are ripping up any white man they come across. Crazy — that's what you are. Now me — I'm getting my wagons loaded up and making tracks — before the weather breaks. Worst we can do is sit and get snowed in. Then we'd be sitting ducks for their arrows and axes."

Tom caught his arm as he brushed past. "You got a gun I can have?"

The storekeeper may have been in a rush, but not enough to ignore money. "You got $20?"

Tom went through his pockets. "Less than ten."

The storekeeper paused. He could feel the determination in the hand gripping his arm. He looked at the whitened knuckles and then up at Tom's face. "There's one in back, with shells. Take what you need by way of provisions too. I can't get it all on my wagons. What's left behind will go to the Indians anyways." The hardness suddenly disappeared from his eyes. Who was he to cut the last thread of hope? "What the hell — there's even a spare horse you can have. But, mister, you're plumb crazy."

★ ★ ★

When Tom left later in the morning Walla Walla was deserted. As he'd prepared himself he had been aware of the constant creak of wheels as wagon upon wagon left the settlement. So now he was alone. Alone in a strange inhospitable country. But at least he was well equipped. At the storekeeper's invitation he'd helped himself to clean, dry clothes, a leather jacket, fur overcoat, a rifle, two handguns and a warbag full of provisions.

Seemingly in little time he reached once more the site of the massacre. There had been a slight fall of snow but the tracks left by the large group of Indians were still clear. He'd started out with a horse but from this point on the animal was likely to be more of a hindrance than help so he pointed it in the direction of Walla Walla and slapped its rump.

He ascended without break until dusk. With the night wind coming down harsh there was no substitute for shelter and before the light disappeared altogether he found himself a small cave and took supper of hardtack.

Early next morning he pulled himself stiffly out of his bivouac and surveyed the terrain. During the night there had been a considerable fall of snow and the Indians' tracks were now obliterated. He set off in the direction that he remembered seeing them the night before.

As the morning progressed he caught sight of caribou and elk but nothing of consequence until midday. His eyes were tiring with snow glare when he saw two figures moving across the top of a ridge. He couldn't see details but he assumed they had to be Indians. They could only be Indians.

It was Indians that he wanted to see — but he didn't want to be picked off by a couple of sentries, if that's what they were, before he got to the main encampment with a chance to state his piece.

He glanced over his shoulder at his backtrail. The ascending line of churned snow that marked his passage stood out against the virgin whiteness. Those two redskins up there — there was no way they could avoid seeing the tracks he had made. Worse: whichever direction he took in search of refuge, his travails would be signposted in a most obvious fashion.

He would just have to accept the inevitable. He swung hard right and made for a clump of Douglas fir. Beneath the umbrella of trees there was less snow on the ground and he could make better headway. After a few minutes running he heard a shout to his rear. They had finally seen his tracks. He maintained his pace for another fifty yards, then paused, breathing heavily, and looked back. He could just see them. They had reached the marks of his passage and were looking into the forest.

With the disturbed snow clearly indicating his every move he reckoned there was to be no escape. And two seasoned warriors against one inexperienced settler . . .

If he had a chance it lay in surprise. But how? He leaned against a tree to steady himself and levered the rifle in readiness for a last-ditch shoot-out. As he waited for them to make sizeable targets he glanced around him. Nothing but trees and virgin snow. Virgin snow! There was a way he could use that to his advantage. Tracks? He'd give 'em tracks!

He took to running again, further into the temporary safety of the forest. Making sure he was out of view he started to run more erratically but gradually he curved round, the trees obscuring him from the Indians. After about ten minutes he'd completed the circle, right round, until he reached the tracks of his pursuers. He deliberately overshot the marks for a dozen yards or so, and then ran backwards to the crossing point. Still moving backwards he went down their common trail. Clearing the trees again he turned about, keeping within the tracks. Yes, that would confuse them. It wouldn't fool them indefinitely, but the ruse could give him some headway.

Eventually he reached the spot where the Indians had met up with his tracks and he retraced those of his pursuers back to the top of the ridge. He crested the summit and before dropping from view he glanced back. The Yakimas, if that's what they were, were still in the forest. His last ditch stratagem had worked, at least temporarily.

He felt some diversionary smugness as he progressed downward through the trees unseen by his pursuers. Hey, a humble Scot had out-foxed redmen — on their own ground!

An hour later, tired and cold, he spotted smoke curling up from the trees further up the mountain. It had to be the Indian encampment. He fell against a tree, exhausted, and closed his eyes for a few seconds respite. It was the first time his vigilance had slackened since he'd set out from Walla what seemed a lifetime ago.

But in such circumstances vigilance needed to be absolute. Hardly had his lids fallen when he heard a strange swishing sound behind him and before he realized what was happening he felt a hot searing pain at the back of his neck.

He grimaced with the effort of turning. His blood, already cold, ran even colder as he did so. With soul-piercing whoops two befeathered Indians were bearing down upon him, clouds of powdery snow billowing out. With one hand he wrenched at the arrow which, although wafted from its intended target by the mountain wind, had impaled him by his clothing to the tree. With the other hand he raised the already-levered rifle and fired. But in his haste the slug did no more than bring a shower of snow from the foliage.

He managed to free himself just as the nearest attacker closed in on him with raised axe. He lifted his arms instinctively. Then he knew no more.

3

WHEN he awoke he was sure he was in hell. Only in hell could there be such pain. The first pain that ripped him from the salve of unconsciousness was in his right temple. Then he remembered that the last thing he had seen was an upraised axe plunging down on him. The saving grace had been that the blunt edge had been foremost. Otherwise his head would be more than paining; it would be in two distinct pieces. Next he sensed the raw groove made across his neck by the arrow. As his awareness intensified he discovered he was suspended from a tripod of timber beams. His thonged wrists were numb.

It was difficult for him to move his head but he could make out other tripods on either side. At least he was

31

more alive than their burdens. Hanging from each were near-frozen carcases of caribou. As his mind took stock of the situation he contemplated the question as to whether he was to be a Christ or a Barrabas.

He didn't know how long he had been hanging there. He surmised it couldn't have been long. Without his thick overclothes he would surely have been as dead as the meat around him, dangling as he was on the top of the world at the mercy of the autumn winds.

Then the tripod began to shake rhythmically as though someone was shinning up one of the timbers that supported him. Then there was an Indian close, cutting through the main thong above him. He was conscious of the man's breath, strange to his nostrils, when the thong parted. He crumpled as he hit the icy ground and was too numb to get up of his own accord. He sensed being dragged away from the exposed summit.

Like a puppet he was supported before a tepee amidst a gathering of what he supposed were Yakima tribesfolk. His legs still without capability, he dropped on to his knees. People jabbered in an unknown tongue, the Sahaptin dialect he guessed of which he'd heard miners speak. Eventually an old man emerged, swathed in furs with a multitude of eagle feathers hanging from a headpiece.

The man spoke slowly, deliberately. "You interest me, white man." The words were English. "Why you come? You brave, or a fool? Or maybe you scout for white soldier."

Tom pulled on all his resources and spoke with difficulty. "I am from the East. I came with wagons. Indians attacked."

The man nodded as though the statement had some meaning for him.

"My wife was taken," Tom continued. "I've come to take her back."

The man nodded once more. After some contemplation he spoke in the strange tongue and Tom was dragged away to another tepee. The deerskin flap was pulled back and he was thrust inside. His eyes, with nothing to look at but blinding snow for so long, were not accustomed to the sudden darkness, so he could make nothing of the interior. But he recognized the voice.

"Tom!" It was Kate.

"Kate," he croaked.

He felt her reaching for him but they were pulled apart.

"What have they done to you?" she screamed. The same question with regard to her was in his throat but he had no chance to voice it or make any reply as he was dragged back outside to the chief.

Someone spoke in dialect to the chief. The old man nodded once more. "So the woman did belong to you."

"Christ, yes. She's my wife, for God's sake."

The chief was unaffected by Tom's emotion. "She now belongs to the tepee of Quinquian, my son."

34

"I said she's my wife!" Tom shouted, his strength gradually returning.

"The white man does not understand many things," the chief proclaimed. "He not understand the having of slaves." He waved his hand expansively. "Nor does he understand that all this land belong to redman. He want to take land."

The man beside the chief was grinning. He whispered in the old man's ear. The chief spoke again. "My son, Quinquian, say he prepared to fight for his new slave. Are you prepared to fight for woman that you call wife?"

Tom was no fighting man but he had no choice. "Yes."

"Then let it be."

The ring of people widened and one man cut through Tom's wrist bonds while another tied a longer thong to Tom's left ankle. The other end was fixed to the right ankle of the man identified as Quinquian.

Tom rubbed his wrists vigorously. Despite his acquiescence he foresaw only one result from the contest. Minutes later a knife was thrust into the ground at his feet.

"That is to be your weapon when I lower my arm," the chief explained.

The two men faced each other. Quinquian had stripped to the waist. His brown skin seemed impervious to the cold wind cutting across the encampment. His face mirrored his anticipation.

The chief's arm dropped. Both men pulled their knives out from the ground before them and began circling each other, the one menacing, the other defensive.

Quinquian made the first direct lunge and Tom was congratulating himself on avoiding the first thrust when he realized it was a feint. And it had been done for a purpose: Quinquian used it to give himself the opportunity to lean down and grab the cord that joined them. Before Tom could step back in counter-balance Quinquian yanked the thong pulling Tom's leg from under him. As he fell heavily on his back his opponent leapt on him with the ferocity of a mountain lion.

Both men gripped the wrist of the other's knife hand and they locked together in a vibrating stalemate. But the Indian was clearly the stronger and Quinquian's blade sliced the cold air nearer and nearer to Tom's face. The white man writhed energetically and managed eventually to yank himself free and roll clear. Both men were on their feet again. But Tom had learned his lesson and he too now had a length of the bonding thong coiled around his hand to prevent his opponent jerking him once more from his feet.

Again Quinquian took the initiative, swinging his blade in a vicious arc which sliced open the front of Tom's jacket. The redman brought the knife around on the back swing with equal success. But the success was his undoing. The blade caught momentarily in Tom's fast shredding jacket. In the split second of his opponent's fumbling

Tom coiled the joining thong around the Indian's neck and tightened it. Quinquian dropped his blade and fell forward using both hands in his attempt to release the throttling coil. Tom maintained the pressure although he didn't know what his chances were if he killed the son of the chief.

They stayed that way for many seconds, Quinquian's gurglings becoming fainter, Tom still holding his own blade.

Suddenly a command was given. The voice was frail and could hardly be heard above the noises of the circled onlookers. Despite its quietness it had significance for the members of the tribe and thus was heard — in the same way that the light splintering of a twig can be heard by the attuned ear of a man of the forest. Indeed, Tom was only aware of it because of the hush that fell on the spectators. He looked back to see the chief make a lateral movement with his arm and repeat the command.

Tom guessed it to be Indian dialect for 'stop' and relinquished his grip on his opponent's throat. He stood back as the Indian, now free, rolled on to his back grabbing lungfuls of the icy air. No one did anything and no one spoke until Quinquian was composed enough to turn, a hang-dog expression on his face, to see what his father had further to command. Then the young Indian rose in response to the words that did come, picking up his fallen knife and cutting the thong that had joined the two combatants.

The chief continued in faltering English. He was clearly addressing the white man. "I said that I did not know whether you were fool or man of courage. The two can be so close. You come to strange land. You clever — I hear how you out-fox my scouts in the wood. Then, for your woman, you walk into camp of many-number redman. I not think you are fighter, yet you prepared to fight many-scalp warrior. You are man of courage." There was a pause. Then, "Woman — she your squaw. No slave to Yakima."

As he spoke his extended arm moved slightly, adding chiefly emphasis to his words. "You go white chief Olympia. Tell: Yakima not take white man's treaty. White man will not divide redman land. Tribes will have pow-wow. Redman divide redman land."

Tom was not concerned with the politics of the situation. "And I take my wife?"

The wizened fingers rose skyward. "The snow gods are here. You leave squaw in warm Yakima tepee. She be safe for when you return. There is Sketana's word on that."

The relief was apparent in Tom's face. "I accept your word, Chief. You are an honourable man. But I still wish to take my wife now."

"The decision is yours. She is your property. In any case, we give furs and blankets for your journey. Food, too."

The treatment of the white man and his squaw changed from that moment on. They ate at the camp-fire as equals to the redman.

Tom found himself ripping into caribou meat alongside his former opponent. Quinquian's English was better than his father's. Tom discovered that he'd been taught at a missionary school and what English his father knew had been passed on by his son. After a long conversation Tom plucked up courage to ask, "Why are the Indians suddenly attacking the white men?"

"As my father has said, they are taking our lands."

"Yes. But it is my understanding that it is only by treaty agreed by yourselves."

"Pah. It is one-sided bargain. He take our land, give back small piece."

"But you receive payment — commodities and money."

Quinquian scoffed. "I know the meaning of the white man's money." He tapped his forehead in the universal gesture of showing understanding. "We are given what is called — annuities.

41

It strange word but it sound good. I make calculation. Each Indian is going to get fifty cents a year. You know the meaning of fifty cents? It not buy much in white man's store. Is that worth parting with our birthright?"

Tom shook his head. As a newcomer he hadn't realized the deals were that raw.

Quinquian continued, "And I tell you one more thing. White man make his mark on treaty — but his mark is no good until treaty ratified by white man's council of elders — what he calls Congress in the East. That can be a full season. In all that time, white man can change his mind. Even if white elders ratify they are not concerned to see that all details are followed. I have heard of it happening to other tribes. On the other hand, redman put mark on treaty — it is binding immediately. He, no change mind. And he sees that all tribe members are honourable. Well, before that, we change our mind."

He wiped grease from his mouth.

"Many whites come to land *before* treaty ratified. We do not kill. We send back. So, they return with guns and fight. So now we kill. You take my father's message to governor in Olympia. Yakima not ratify treaty. We ourselves divide up land among the seven tribes."

* * *

The next day, after a night in their own warm tepee in which they had slept soundly with little exchange, Tom and Kate set off down the mountain. His warbag was filled with Indian food, and Kate wore a fur shawl given by Quinquian.

After an hour they stopped to rest on a ledge. A light snowfall had begun and they watched the flakes drifting down into the great void below them.

Tom took his wife's hand. "Did they ill-treat you?"

She paused as if choosing her words carefully. "Not in a violent way."

His face tightened and he looked at the fur shawl wrapped round her slight figure, the gift of the chief's son. "Were you . . . molested?"

She paused even longer before answering this time. "Quinquian . . . took me . . . once."

Tom covered his eyes with his hand.

"He claimed me as his woman," she continued.

"God," he said with a tremor. "Does that justify it?"

"No, of course not."

He exhaled noisily. "I had him under my knife. I wish I'd killed him."

She put an arm weakly around his shoulders. "Things may have turned out differently if you had."

★ ★ ★

As the day wore on the snow got worse and the temperature dropped. Kate got rapidly weaker. Although it was not yet dark Tom decided to camp for the night as his wife was shivering and having difficulty breathing. He found the cave he'd used previously. Once inside he tried to get her to eat some of the caribou meat given them by the Indians but she showed no interest. He tried her with some of the hardtack which he had remaining from his outward trip, but she had no interest in food from any source.

After a long time he did manage to force her to take some strengthening caribou marrow supplied by the Yakima.

He felt her brow — she was shivering and, despite the cold, sweating profusely at the same time. He got more and more worried as the night wore on, her shivering becoming more violent and her breathing increasingly difficult. He built up the fire and, with his precious bundle in his arms, he fought off sleep until eventually fatigue forced itself upon him.

When he awoke, his wife's shaking had stopped. For a moment he was glad. But then he realized the absence of movement was complete. She was not even breathing.

He held her close for a long time. He didn't want to leave her. His Kate. He looked at her in his arms and thought of the warm tepee from which he had insisted on taking her. The tears froze on his cheeks.

A long time later, a lonely figure stumbled downwards through the drifts.

4

HE ploughed on through the snow, his mind numbed by events as his body was numbed by the cold. The dreams he had shared with Kate of a new beginning in a new land were shattered. His exhausting travails and the trauma of the death of his loved one compounded to plunge him into a pit of despair, despair increasingly tinged with bitterness. In the last few days he had come to hate this country, its violence, the snow and ice. He thought of the heather-clad glens they had left behind. The braes themselves would now be snow-covered but he thought of them with nothing but fondness. Somehow the terrain of his homeland was without the harshness he had come to find in this vast, wild, untamed country. He sorely wished to return home but he had little money, certainly none for the return passage.

It wasn't until he reached Tacoma that he remembered Sketana's request. His brain still numbed by his ordeal, he passed on the chief's message to the authorities. They asked questions and he told them his story. They sought information on the location of the camp and numbers of braves. He told them what he could but his mind was on his own circumstances. They sympathized, gave him a few dollars to tide him over but they had their own concerns.

He used the money to buy himself accommodation and hot food and then lay on his bunk thinking on his next step. He considered taking up work on the western seaboard with the intent of raising enough money to buy a sail ticket home. But, through the frost-covered glass of his hotel window, he could see the constant flow of wagons coming in from the hinterland, over-laden with the salvaged belongings of homesteaders who had uprooted themselves. He'd heard their talk of new atrocities. Like him most were penniless and couldn't afford to buy sea passage. He didn't have to be an economic philosopher to see that there would soon be a glut of labour in the locality and the resulting rock-bottom rates of pay would mean he might have to work for years at some back-breaking job to save enough to get out.

Furthermore the talk amongst the community was of impending all-out war with the Indians. That meant there would be pressure on all able-bodied men to take up arms and join the ranks. He was no coward, he'd proved that to himself; but this wasn't his war. Moreover, having been face-to-face with the people the white men called savages, he knew they had a case. And they weren't savages; they had their own codes, their own honour. No point in fighting battles when your heart was half on the other's side.

The prospect of becoming embroiled in a war which was not his, or of toiling in a place that already had sad memories for him, prompted him to dismiss the option of staying in the territory.

From that his thoughts went to travelling north into Canada where, he had heard, there was less conflict between the races. But, shivering under his sougans, he dismissed that option on the grounds that conditions that-aways would be colder still. So it was, after a few days' rest, he packed a warbag and left Tacoma to journey south.

During his travelling he kept himself to himself, stayed in his own world. It was a sadness the like of which he had never known. He felt alone and facing a void. His unhappiness was compounded with guilt. Kate had died because of him and his decision to leave the Indian camp. On reflection he realized he should have trusted the redmen. Despite their attacking whites, actions which now he truly thought had justification, they were honourable. The Scots couple had been offered shelter through the winter by the redmen and he, in his pig-headedness, had refused. The consequence had been the death of Kate. No one's fault but his own.

In order to survive he worked at odd jobs along the way, grateful at least for the rising temperature that came with more southern latitudes. He swamped saloons, served a spell in a dry goods store and worked stock on several occasions. Days passed into weeks, weeks into months. The longest he stayed in one place was when he helped a fellow build a barn in Nevada. But in none of the occupations did he open up or make friends. By all those with whom he came in contact he was seen as the man who never smiled and, whenever he'd earned enough dollars to move on, he did so.

Months became seasons, and seasons moved on to a new calendar. He didn't know where he was going, what he was going to do. It was like riding the current of some uncharted waterway: aware of being swept along the river of life but unaware of the destination.

★ ★ ★

Into his second season of travelling he found employment on a horse ranch in New Mexico. He took to the work and stayed a year with the outfit. For the first time in a long spell he found a little peace of mind. The job was more than just straining his muscles, gave him something to concentrate on. He learned basics about horse-lore: how to saddlebreak a bronc, the different breeds, what to look for when buying stock, how to tend common illnesses and injuries.

Being raised in the glens the only stock animals he knew had been sheep. The horse was a whole new world for him. He learned about the nature of the animal and its habits, and discovered how each had its own individual character. Some were uppity, others had a sense of fun. What he liked about the horse was that he was a plain-spoke animal: if he was a mean critter he'd let you know it from the outset.

Had none of that deviousness that could characterize two-legged critters.

But he became fiddle-footed once more. Like he couldn't let too much grass grow under his feet, feet that were now accustomed to leather western-style riding-boots. At least, when he finally left the outfit he had a good horse under him, a three-year-old mare, part range stock, part Appaloosa; and he carried a sizeable billfold in his pocket.

The man who waved so-long and rode away was changing in other ways too, besides his mode of dress. Without his knowledge his way of talking was gradually changing. With its flattened 'a', his original Scots accent had already been first cousin to the American style of speech. Now with a spattering of new vocabulary it was becoming less distinguishable from that of other folk on the American continent.

5

SEVERAL years had passed since his journey from the cold northlands. He had fetched up in Texas, found himself an unclaimed piece of land and established a smallholding from scratch. Nothing much, a shack he had built unaided, out-houses and corrals. A tight fence marked off a piece of pasture. He had chickens, a couple of pigs and a milk-cow. Just enough for him to live independently, his only companion a dog that had latched on to him.

Some kind of Bollenbiesser, the dog was of medium size but heavy in build and of daunting appearance, taking it upon himself to be a staunch guardian of his new home. His looks however belied his character and he had settled at Tom's side as a faithful friend. Tom didn't have to think long for a name for the animal. With his broad forehead, short pushed-up nose and slobbering undershot jaw, the critter reminded Tom of an ugly bare-knuckle fighter he had seen on the streets of Glasgow who, under the name of Butch, took on all-comers. The dog seemed to relish the label and that was that.

In the nearby town which Tom visited as rarely as he could, he was seen as a recluse. During his exchanges for trade he kept conversation to a minimum, told nobody about himself. They knew nothing about him save for what his fading accent told them. Apart from such dealings his only contact with the outside world was the newspapers he bought from time to time and kept in a yellowing stack in a corner. From them he had learned that it had taken a three-year war to defeat the Indians back in Washington Territory, during which dozens of their leaders were hanged. Then he had read that the tribes had been herded into reservations and their lands confiscated and opened up for the settlers. He was glad to have been out of the whole shebang.

Satisfied that he could meet his physical needs and still have time left over in the day, his mind turned to expanding. It was then he decided to put his apprentice knowledge of horses into practice. In time he'd got himself six horses running in his extended pasture. The previous fall had seen his first delivery of a foal.

Late one day, his major chores over, he was smoking his pipe in a chair by the fire when he heard the dog barking. He listened: there were hooves, then a knock at the door. He opened it to face a man wearing a black derby. He vaguely recognized the face.

"Ain't gonna have my arm off, is he?" the man said, having to bend down to placate the enthusiastic dog.

"He's friendly enough," Tom said, "just as long you don't make any quick movements." He didn't mean it, but he saw no harm in maintaining the pretence that he had a vicious animal on the premises. "Inside, Butch," he said, and the dog obeyed, standing with his stumpy tail wagging behind his master.

"Mr Connor, isn't it?" the man went on to enquire.

"Yeah."

"I'm your neighbour, Eli Weber."

"Oh yeah, what do you want?" His greeting was abrupt. None of that "What can I do for you, pardner?" stuff for the loner.

The man was not put off by the cold response. "It's Independence Day, Mr Connor."

The occasion meant nothing to the Scot. "So what?"

"Well, the folks are having a hoedown in Ryan's barn tonight," the man continued. "You'd be mighty welcome there."

Tom shook his head. "Ain't the kinda thing I take pleasure in."

"We figured you'd say that."

"We? Who's we?"

"Your neighbours. All your neighbours. We had a jaw-boning session to arrange the thing and when your name was mentioned for an invite the feeling was you wouldn't be interested."

"The feeling was right, Mr Weber."

"Yes, sir, we figured that and the feeling was we should press on and invite you anyways. Fact is, we'll be calling for you in two hours as we pass by on the way to the shindig. We wanna see you ready at that time and raring to go."

"You'll be calling in vain."

"We'll still be calling."

Before Tom could say anything else Weber turned on his heel and was heading for his horse. "And we ain't taking no for an answer," he shouted back as he mounted up. "The boys and their missuses can be mighty persuasive. Just make sure you're ready."

As the man rode off, Tom grunted and closed the door. "Meddling busybodies," he said to himself as he settled back in his chair. But his pipe had gone out and, when he relighted it, it tasted bitter. He tried to relax but couldn't settle. "Hoedown shmo-down," he said aloud after a while and went to the stove to cook up a meal. But when it came to eating he couldn't finish it, his stomach wound up like a drum. Hell, he didn't like being interfered with, didn't cotton to folks nosing into his affairs.

He knew his own temperament. Now it had been triggered, he was going to be in this ill-humour for a spell. If they called like the man said, he'd send them off with a flea in their ear. But that wouldn't be the end of it; the resentment would increase and linger through the night. It would spur him to take liquor, as he often did, but he knew that would only serve to bring back painful memories. Judas Priest, what made folks be interfering like this? All he wanted was to be left alone.

He left the unfinished meal and crossed to the cracked mirror on the wall where he examined his features. He'd not been concerned with his appearance for a long, long time and it was a strange face that peered back at him. Around the eyes, across his temple and beneath the stubble round his mouth there were creases he hadn't noticed before. And some grey hairs in the unkempt locks. He exhaled noisily in irritation at having his enclosed world invaded.

He sat around some more and worked himself up into a lather. Only way to scuttle this irritation was face it. He looked at the clock; still had time for the necessaries. He heated water and took a tub to rid his body of his usually permanent smell of chores and sweat. He rubbed himself down vigorously, then shaved. He cursed when he nicked himself, unaccustomed to such close preening. The dog lay still by the fire, head down, chin on his paws, but eyes following his master in his strange movements.

Then it occurred to the man he

didn't have any what he'd heard folks call Sunday-go-to-meeting clothes. Grunting irritably to himself in his search through his meagre wardrobe, holding up a shirt here, examining pants for tears there, he eventually pulled himself into a set of working clothes. He appraised his garb. There were darnings but rents were at a minimum and at least the stuff was clean. Judas Priest, what more could the do-gooders ask for?

The dog barked before Tom heard the racket outside. Horses, wheels, voices. He opened the door. It was Eli Weber. "You coming by horse, Mr Connor?" he asked, fending off the welcoming dog. "Or wanna jump on our buggy. We kept room for you."

Tom wasn't prepared for such complicated questions.

"Never know," Weber went on. "You drink too much and you ain't gonna get back unless your hoss knows his way home." He laughed and looked back. "S'happened before, ain't it, Aggie?"

There were two women, a couple of kids and another man in the wagon. One of the women shouted back endorsing the man's observation.

"I'll ride alongside on my hoss if it's all the same," Tom said, not cottoning to the idea of being shoved up against a wagon-load of strangers. Also, it would free him to return of his own accord when he'd had enough of the shenanigans, which wouldn't be long.

They waited while he saddled up. When he was mounted Weber made introductions and they headed out into the darkness of the evening.

* * *

The place was just as he expected. Noisy and full of jabbering people. Red, white and blue banners decorated the beams and walls. A trio of musicians stood on a makeshift stage constructed of planking on barrels and the combination of fiddle, banjo and mandolin made sounds strange to his ears. He hoped to take refuge in the abundant drink that was provided but the party with whom he had arrived would have none of it and soon inveigled him into joining in the community dancing. The American style of 'cavorting', as he called it, was new to him but the crofters' ceilidhs he had experienced in his youth ensured that, when forced, at least he wasn't afraid to put one foot in front of the other. Taking his cue from the others he soon got a rough idea of where to direct his big feet and when to stand back clapping.

The rare times when he did manage to grab a drink and retire to the edge of the dancing area, it was not the haven for which he hoped. He stood awkwardly, very conscious of eyes upon him. Folks were interested in the man who had finally come out of his shell and there was no end to the stream of revellers who took the liberty of introducing themselves and asking him questions. These Americans were sure pushy folk. In terms of discomfort there was little to choose between making a spectacle of himself on the floor and being besieged by a barrage of questions from strangers.

He was grateful when there was a change in activity. The dancing ceased for a spell and folk took it in turns to clamber up on the stage to sing. The songs were unknown to him but clearly familiar to many of the revellers as they joined in the choruses. Most of the songs were in English, or what passed for English this side of the great ocean, but now and then there would be a song in a foreign tongue reflecting the varied make-up of the settlers.

For the first time in the evening he was left in peace and was able to take a few drinks. The stuff was strong and soon a cocoon of alcohol lessened his unease. So much so, that he began to evaluate the proceedings. What was this all about? A bunch of ex-colonials celebrating the breaking of ties with the mother country. The mother country, indeed. It was his mother country!

Alcohol has different effects on men. For some, inhibitions are lowered so that their behaviour becomes unmannered, particularly with respect to the fair sex. Others are made more aggressive and seek fights. Alcohol always had the same effect on Tom, as it did back in the cabin, in making him melancholic. He began to think of Kate, of what might have been. Then, as always, of their homeland. He longed to hear the pipes again. To see the scarlet tunics marching down Princes Street.

He was hauled out of his reverie by Eli Weber pulling on his arm. A pathway, lined with expectant faces, had been cleared for him to the rickety stage. He was being invited to sing!

"Oh, nay, fellers," he said, the drink having brought the accent of his origins to the surface. Despite his protestation he was guided to the rostrum and helped on to the platform. Suddenly he found himself facing a hushed sea of faces.

There was no way out. They wanted a song. His mind went blank. Then he thought, I'll gi' 'em a song. He turned ungainly to the musicians and nodded. "OK, fellers, I'd appreciate some melodious support here." He turned back to the crowd. "Feel free to join in, folks, if you please."

Then he raised his glass, belched, apologized, cleared his throat and began to sing. For the first time in the whole evening the place became deathly quiet. His rendition of 'God save the Queen' was greeted with absolute silence. But he was enjoying himself. If he had had a Union Jack he would have waved it. However, at the end of the first verse he staggered some and was saved from falling by a couple of the musicians who took the opportunity to help him off the stage before he could continue his blasphemy.

Against a background of tufting and whispering he managed to make his way unaided to the fringes once more. From then on he found himself alone, smiling smugly at folk through bleary eyes. Hadn't he tried to tell folk he was an individual? Well, now he'd shown them. They wanted to talk; well now he'd given them something to talk about. Brighten their parochial lives. He was pleased with himself; now he could leave this shindig without being pestered.

But no, why should he? At last he was beginning to enjoy himself.

He made his way outside and stood in the dark. He took a swig of his drink as someone returned the place behind him to normality by singing some vaguely familiar music-hall song. He leant against the wall, groaned in something resembling contentment and stared at the stars. He was there a long time before he realized he was not alone. In the darkness he sensed there was someone near. Yes, a little further along there was a woman, girl, somebody feminine. He could smell the lavender water above the animal smells of the corral.

He raised his glass. "Hi, there, lassie," he said into the darkness.

"Good evening, sir." The voice was low, hesitant.

Moving nearer he could make out a small, slim shape. "Mind if I join you, miss?"

"No."

"Name's Connor. Tom Connor."

"Yes, I know. I've heard folks talking about you. Pleased to make your acquaintance. I'm Mary Dickens."

"If I had my hat on I would doff it," he said drunkenly. "But as I ain't, I can't." He laughed as though he'd told the funniest joke of the week. He composed himself as best he could. "So you know something of me?"

"I know you are a man who has put a cat amongst some pigeons."

For a moment he didn't understand. Then he said, "Oh, back there. Hah, reckon it's a long time since they heard that song!" He laughed again, then became serious. "Say, you think I've upset folks?"

"Some. But most will understand. A goodly portion of them have come from somewhere in Europe."

"You're not European," he observed.

"No. First generation."

They talked inconsequentially for a while, until a man came out in search of her. A bearded guy with a limp.

"Nice to have met you, Miss Mary," Tom said, raising an imaginary hat as she was escorted back into the barn. He thought he saw her throw the briefest of smiles at him as she passed through the lit doorway.

He crossed to the corral and leant on the fence. A couple of horses came to investigate and he rubbed their muzzles. He had grown fond of horses. "You fellers would be the best company I've met all night," he mused, "if I hadn't 'a met Miss Mary."

6

ELI WEBER'S advice about having a horse that knew its way home had been no idle comment. Tom awoke late the next morning. Unlike his usual habit the dog didn't move when Tom finally greeted the day with something sembling consciousness. The perplexed animal had licked his master's face to no avail several times since sun-up and now had lost any interest.

After a wash and shave Tom deferred attendance to his normal tasks and rode out to the Ryan's spread. His action was spurred by two objectives. The first was to apologize to his host for any offence he had given by the inappropriateness of his musical offering.

He came upon Ryan working out in his fields. The man stopped in his labour and looked up with the face of a genial cod fish.

"Well, neighbour," he said after Tom had explained his concern, "you'll have made some enemies, that's for sure." Then his rubbery lips bent into a wry smile. "But nothing that requires pistols at dawn. Don't fret. You'll be forgiven in time. We're a few miles west of the thirteen colonies."

The other thing Tom wanted to ask was about Mary Dickens. But on the ride over he had decided against making enquiries. The freedom facilitated by the previous evening's alcohol had now evaporated and bumping up and down on his horse in the cold light of day he had given some thought to the implications of his asking after a woman. It could be interpreted as something more than it was. All he knew was that he had enjoyed talking to her, she had been a brief light in his darkness. But it couldn't be more than that to him; and the gossips of the area would certainly ascribe something

71

more serious to the news of him making enquiries.

So he didn't ask after Mary, just saw off his meeting with Ryan with a neighbourly chat, then returned home. Thus it was he put her out of his mind and as the days and weeks passed his thoughts turned less and less to the pretty girl in the shadows. It was well over a month before he saw her again. He'd gone into town for supplies and just as he was entering a dry goods store, he caught sight of her sitting on the box seat of a wagon along the street.

In the store he ordered a bag of coffee but his mind was not wholly on the transaction and he had to be reminded to pick up his change. She was still there when he emerged once more into the daylight. As he deposited the package into his saddle-bag he pondered on the girl he had been trying to forget. She was sitting there, large as life, pretty as a picture. His instincts lost their fight with his intellect, and he moved down the street. He presented himself before her and doffed his hat. "Good day to you, Miss Mary."

She laughed gently. "You have a hat today."

She talked so quiet that he had difficulty hearing her. Even so he didn't understand the reference. "Nice to set eyes on you again," he went on.

"And a pleasure to see you again, Mr Connor," she whispered.

"You've remembered my name. That is a good sign."

"A good sign of what, pray?"

"That you have not completely forgotten me."

She looked up at the sky. "Some say there is going to be rain in a while."

"It sure is needed."

"What's needed?" a strange voice interposed. It belonged to a bearded man in corduroy breeches arriving on the scene laden with a large bag of flour.

Tom noted he had a limp. "Here, allow me to help you," he said, taking a grip of the heavy burden.

"I was just saying it's good news about the rain," he said, after he had helped the man sling the bag on to the back of the buckboard, "The name's Connor. Tom Connor."

The man appraised the speaker and chuckled. "Say, you're the English feller who treated the folks to a sing-song at the hop back apiece."

"Scots," Tom corrected.

"Well, what's a Scotchman doing talking weather to our Mary?"

"Just passing the time of day, mister." Tom summoned up courage and turned to the girl. "I'd really like to know if you're spoke for."

"You's a blunt kinda feller, ain't you, Mr Connor," the man said. "That ain't a right question to ask a girl."

"I apologize if I've broken etiquette. Is it proper for me to ask you if your daughter's spoke for?"

The man chuckled again and scratched at his beard. "Ain't my daughter, Mr Connor. My missus's sister." He turned to the girl. "Figure this feller's making out he wants to come a-calling on you, Mary. What do you have to say?"

The girl looked shy and whispered something to the questioner.

"Seems you're seen as on the square," the man said. "Tomorrow evening suit you, six o'clock? You can eat with us. You'll like it. Ruth, my missus, is the best cook this side of the Red River." He stuck out his hand. "Name's Ned Burgess."

"Pleased to make your acquaintance, Mr Burgess," Tom said as the two men shook hands.

"You can call me Ned," the other said and gave the location of their quarters.

"That's mighty kind," Tom said. "I look forward to it."

The man heaved himself up into the driving seat and without another word the buckboard moved out.

★ ★ ★

The meal went well and Tom learned Mary had been orphaned on the trek west and had fallen into the hands of Mormons who had seen to her raising out in Utah. Worked in near-slave conditions and destined to be married Mormon-style she had hidden in a wagon leaving the territory. She had sought refuge with her sister and husband. "That's why she don't talk much," Ned said as the two men took a smoke out on the verandah after the meal. "Mormon women are raised to be quiet and take orders from the menfolk. Even when she talks it's quieter'n a church mouse."

"She sure is a comely lass," Tom observed.

Ned drew on his cigarette and studied the smoke. "Gives sign she enjoys your company too." He paused and reflected some more. "Listen, seeing's she ain't got no folks and she's living with us, I figure I'm the only one looking out for her. What she's been through she needs a little looking after. So, although

I ain't much older than her, I sees it as my duty to act like a pa, leastways in the matter of menfolk. You can get your brain round that, can't you, Tom?"

"Surely can."

"Mary's a mite on the plain side but there's been a few sniffing round. But I didn't fancy their cut so I poured water on their tails. Now you're different. Although I don't know you, I do know you been in these parts for a few years."

"Four."

"Whatever. Anyways, during that time you ain't given nobody no cause to think you're a bad un. Just seems you're a guy with his own reasons for keeping hisself to hisself. Ain't nothing wrong in that. All folks is different. Me, myself, I thinks you're on the square. Tell me, you got serious intentions towards the gal?"

"To be truthful, I haven't got any plans yet awhiles."

"Yeah, suppose it is early days."

"No, it's more than that." Tom proceeded to tell him about coming to the United States, about Kate, what had happened and the resulting difficulty he had of thinking of women.

"Understandable, Tom. Glad you confided in me. Explains a lot about the way you have of keeping out of folks' way. Well, I'll tell you this: as long as Mary takes a shine to you you're welcome to drag your boots in here. You take your time and, if you feel serious, tell me and the missus. Then you can do your courting in your own way."

Tom paid many visits subsequently to the Burgess place and eventually was allowed to take walks with Mary. He told her of his past. His country with its highlands and lowlands. She began to open up and ask questions. He told her of the long voyage to America. But it was when he told of what had befallen the couple in the North-West that she became quiet again. It seemed to him they both had

78

their reason for keeping out of life's mainstream.

* * *

One afternoon they were walking through the sage at the Burgess spread, their hands finger-locked together. Tom felt his heart racing. He'd never thought he could contemplate the notion of another woman after Kate. For years he had kept his own company, not wishing to share any part of his days with another human being. But feelings about Mary had taken hold of him, growing like a seed, stubbornly growing, eventually to blossom uncontrollably within the great void that was his inner world.

At first he'd fought the feelings. The guilt of Kate's death still hung heavy in his heart and the warmth he felt for Mary caused him a new anguish, the guilt of betraying Kate and her memory. Alone in his cabin, he'd wrestled with the dilemma, trying to get Mary out of his mind. He'd talked it over repeatedly with Butch but the mutt had remained resolutely unhelpful.

Slowly an understanding came to him. Mary was a *different* woman. He valued different things about her. There was room in his heart for two women. Mary wasn't replacing Kate. She belonged to another part of his life. Reaching this new understanding brought some peace to his heart, allowing him to feel once more the exhilaration of a new love. And the insecurity that went with it. Hell, he was doing all this soul-searching and he didn't know whether she would have him?

They walked for a long distance in the kind of silence that can be shared by two people who feel at ease with each other. It took him a long time before he broke the silence. He stopped awkwardly, gripping her hand tighter and taking her other hand in his, so that they faced each other.

"We've both been through bad times, Mary. That kind of gives us a common bond. You know what I mean, Mary?"

"I know what you mean, Tom."

He gazed into her eyes, pushing his brain to find the words but it refused to provide them. "I was thinking . . . "

"Yes?"

Eventually he made it. "Would you be partial to you and me being wed?"

She let go of his hands, enclosed his body in her arms and laid her head on his chest. "You know, Tom Connor, I thought you'd never ask."

"Well, would you?"

"I have wished for it more than anything in the world."

"Does this mean we're . . . " He cleared his throat and completed the question, " . . . engaged?"

She chuckled and squeezed him harder. "Of course it does."

7

THEY set the date for the following spring and began the preparations. Once they had named the day, Tom had set about building a substantial log-house. With his crook leg Ned couldn't help much directly but he often visited and brought some members of his crew to add extra hands to the task. And it wasn't long before Tom had a verandahed house fit for his bride. Once the builders' clutter had been taken away and the couple were married and installed, Mary began developing an ambitious flower garden on all four sides.

Occasionally there would be a lump in Tom's throat when he thought of Kate, and how she would have loved this place, the kind of place they would have had together. At such times, usually in the evening when the chores were over and they were sitting on the verandah, Mary might see his eyes glistening but she made no comment.

Tom became more sociable. He and Mary would visit or entertain neighbours. He enjoyed their visits to town, felt the warmth of the welcoming smiles and was pleased at the feeling of being part of a community. When he visited town alone, as he did to buy supplies, he would spend a little time in the saloon, not enough to get drunk but enough for him to enjoy the companionship of the place. It was there that he learned of the coming to prominence of a politician from Illinois, Abraham Lincoln. And of the growing ferment in political affairs.

But one day in the grog-shop he heard matters being discussed which were new to him and a mite disconcerting.

"There won't be a war," an old cracker-barrel philosopher was saying. "The North will never use force to keep us in their damn Union. Anyways, if they do want a ruckus, they won't be any match for Southern fighting men."

Tom had never heard the Union spoken of in terms of being split between north and south.

"Yeah," another said, "but what if the North was to blockade our ports? We'll soon run out of supplies. For a start we ain't got factories. We'll have to buy armaments even."

"No," a third countered. "The South's cotton is too valuable for Europe. They won't let their supplies be cut off by no Yankee blockade. The European powers would threaten to intervene on our side."

"You think they will?" someone asked. "The old countries have got their own problems. I think they'll leave us to get on with it."

"Anyways," the first speaker came back, "don't think it will come to nothing. All the signs are that the North's giving way on the slavery issue for the sake of peace."

"I don't trust that Lincoln. If'n he gets elected to the presidency he'll stand fast on them anti-slavery ideas of his. That's the platform on which his campaign's been based. And he won't countenance the extension of slavery to the Territories. Secession'll be the only answer."

Secession? That was a new word for Tom but he didn't ask its meaning.

The discussion continued. "Nah. He won't get to power. Look at the opposition against him. Anyways, if he does he can't go against the Supreme Court. The Chief Justice has made a ruling prohibiting federal interference in states' affairs on slavery."

On this occasion as on many others, Tom listened to the bar-room statesmen debating the issues but he didn't participate.

For a year the couple wallowed in happiness, a happiness neither of them thought could be exceeded. The excitement of starting a new life together, the warmth of shared feelings.

A slight cloud appeared on the horizon when Tom went to town one day and learned of the election of Lincoln to the presidency, an event which had been quickly followed by the State of South Carolina passing an Ordinance of Secession. There was that word again: secession. It wasn't the word so much that caused unease, it was the fervour with which men spoke when they used it.

He put it at the back of his mind but a few weeks later another word had come to the fore: war. A further six states had withdrawn from the Union and, together with South Carolina, had set up in Alabama what they called the Confederacy. The new country had a president, Davis, and a new flag. The Confederate president had been authorized to raise an army of a hundred thousand men.

Some of the saloon debaters were saying they were willing to go to war over this secession thing. Others said it wouldn't come to that.

"There won't be a war," one old timer had persisted. "Americans won't shoot at Americans. Look how they've let us take over all Federal posts on our side of the lines without any blood-letting." That was true. Soldiers of the new Confederate Army had simply moved into military posts on the territory they claimed without any resistance from the Union garrisons.

Back home he relayed what he had heard to Mary and they talked about it some. Tom said that many believed it wouldn't come to military action but he ended the discussion by stating quite clearly that if war did come it was nothing to do with them. It wouldn't be their war. They had their own lives to think of. Nevertheless he kept his ears open on subsequent visits to the town's debating parlour and always brought home newspapers.

From the newspapers he learned that the Confederacy's commissioners had been in Washington talking to President Lincoln. And, a little later than the other states, Texas had finally joined the Confederacy. Then, worse: guns had been fired at Fort Sumter.

* * *

One year passed, then two. But the war was a distant thing not impinging on their existence. It meant nothing more to the Connors than accounts in newspapers and the scuttlebutt Tom brought home from town. The Mississippi provided a geographical dividing line, a natural feature of terrain which restricted the conflict to the eastern states. So, Tom and Mary lived happily in the little domain that they had carved out for themselves, ignoring the events of the outer world. Tom expanded their spread, making them self-sufficient, and slowly built up his stock of horses.

He regularly saw recruiting officers in town but, after the initial fuss at the beginning of the war, their visits took on almost a social nature with little pressure on civilians. The call to arms had abated with the realization that the western states of the Confederacy — and that meant Texas — were not under immediate military threat from Union forces.

The Confederate Trans-Mississippi Department was under the command of General Kirby Smith who saw his role as a holding one. After forming the nucleus of a fighting force with units such as the Texas Brigade, he built up trading links with European merchants in Mexico using cotton to purchase arms and supplies. He was trying to get resources through to the theatre of war but Federal control of the Mississippi denied all but a trickle to the main body of the Confederacy.

So Texas was having a quiet war. So far.

* * *

Smoke blued the air above the chimney of the Connors' house. Out front Tom was chopping wood, sweat patches showing dark through his homespun shirt. He was swinging his axe with relish. The day before Mary had been to see the town doctor who had confirmed she was expecting a child. The couple had thought they couldn't be happier but now their joy had ascended to new heights.

It was the dog barking that set him to looking along the trail and noting the advance of a couple of riders. He carried on chopping until they were nearer, then he rested on the axe and took stock of them, noting the grey uniforms they both wore. They reined in and the elder of the two dismounted, took off his gauntlets and wiped his brow.

He stood erect, his new uniform already creased and dusty. "Am I addressing Mr Connor, sir?"

"Aye, that's me."

"Figure you know why we're calling."

"I need telling."

The officer gazed around the Connors' lot. "Mighty peaceful out here. But it ain't so peaceful elsewheres. There's a war going on."

"So I hear."

"The Yankees have more of everything: factories to build their guns, an established chain of command, more menfolk for soldiering. So, ain't no picnic for those that wear the grey. That's why the CSA needs first-rate men to volunteer to do a first-rate job. Capable men like yourself."

"Go on."

The man began tapping his thigh with his gauntlets in a steady rhythm. "We're here representing the Texas Brigade to recruit your services."

"Ain't my war, mister."

"And I ain't here for pleading. In such circumstances my task is to acquaint you with the South's need and point out the step an honourable man should take."

"Fancy words, but I ain't a man

of politics. Seems to me politics is just a game played by a small bunch of smart-talking fellers which leads to lots of other fellers getting maimed and killed."

"I'll get to the crunch, Mr Connor. For the last two years the Federals have had enough on their plate out East. So, out here we've had it pretty easy till now. But our intelligence is that the blue-bellies are mounting a special force in New Orleans under General Banks. Its objective is to overrun Texas and set up the US flag on *our* soil. It is now imperative that we enlarge our forces to repel them."

Tom shrugged. "Had to come sometime." He looked at the flat empty countryside around his spread. Couldn't imagine the easterners marching out here. Couldn't imagine why they would want to. "But, like I said, ain't my war."

The younger soldier had stepped down. He was square-faced with a wart on his left cheek. He'd picked a stalk of grass and was probing his teeth with it. "Seems to me, Colonel, the guy's yeller. That's the long and the short of it."

The dog, having quieted and lain down, now began a low growl, sensing the growing tension in the exchanges.

Tom laid down his axe and, fists clenching, he moved towards the young man. "You drop that gunbelt, mister, and I'll show you who's yeller."

"Stow it, Henderson," the elder snapped to his subordinate. "I've told you to leave the jawboning to me." To Connor he said, "With your spirit I can see that you're the kind of man we need, sir. But the aggression you display is better channelled in the cause of the Confederacy. Now that trouble is really on its way several of your neighbours have seen where their duty lies."

Tom returned to his pile of wood and picked up his axe again. "Up to them to make their own decisions." He heard a noise behind him and glanced to see that Mary had come to the door. "All I know is I got a wife to look after and a kid on the way. Ain't no way I'm turning my back on that kind of responsibility."

"So you're refusing to sign up?"

"I'm just declining your offer. But you phrase it anyhow you like."

"And that's your final word?"

"On the matter in hand, yes."

The officer took out a pencil and paper and wrote something down. Then he nodded to his subordinate and the two men mounted. He pulled on his gauntlets and looked down at the farmer from his saddled position. "You can stay around here, doing nothing, ignoring what's happening in the world outside. But you'll only be marking time, Connor. Just remember, those that ain't for us are against us."

With that he mounted up. For a moment the younger soldier remained staring hard at Tom, then pulled himself up into the saddle and the two men rode away. Tom watched them, then laid down his axe and walked up to Mary at the door.

"I'm frightened, Tom," she said.

He encircled her with his arms. "We're gonna be all right. Ain't none of our doing." Familiar feelings of unease returned and he pulled her tight, trying to freeze the moment, the emotion, as though attempting to make it last forever.

8

ALONE hawk hung in the sky. Mary watched it through the window, pausing in her task of scrubbing clothes at the sink. For a moment it was stationary as though part of the sky itself, then it dropped, legs outstretched. She watched it hit the grass and, as it rose again its talons around its prey, she saw riders in the distance. They were riding at a determined gait directly towards the homestead. It was plain they were coming a-calling. As they neared she could see they had a couple of wagons in tow.

She dried her hands and went to the doorway. Some were in grey uniforms, others had everyday work clothes, but she guessed they were all soldiers. She was acquainted enough with affairs to know that the Confederacy couldn't afford uniforms for all its army.

"Howdy, ma'am," the leader said, reining in. He had the three sleeve chevrons which marked him as a sergeant but her knowledge didn't spread to technicalities like that. But she did recognize him as one who had visited earlier. The square-faced young man who had challenged Tom.

"Good day to you," she said coldly.

"Your man about?" he asked, dropping down from his horse.

"No. He's away on business."

"What business is that, ma'am?"

"Horse trading."

The man rubbed the wart on his cheek. "That means he'll be away a spell?"

"Yes." As soon as she'd said it, she felt she had disclosed too much. But her religious upbringing led her to be honest first, the considerations of men's possible deviousness coming a poor second.

"No matter," the sergeant said. "We can handle our business without him."

He took a piece of paper from his tunic. "Official orders, ma'am. The Federals are already heading this way up the Red River. Ain't gonna be long afore all hell breaks loose and we need everything we can get our hands on. We've come to commandeer horses and animal stock for the cause of the Confederacy."

"You can't take our stock!"

"No 'can't' about it, ma'am. Like I said. Official. You can read the orders." He offered the piece of paper and she stepped down from the verandah and took it.

"I'd like you to wait until my husband returns," she said, after she had read it.

"Ain't got the time, ma'am. We've got a lotta ground to cover and you said yourself he'll be away a spell." He turned to his men and motioned towards the big corral.

She dropped her drying cloth and ran towards the fencing. She stood with her arms outstretched against the gate, facing the oncoming soldiers. "You can't take the horses. They're our prime stock."

"All the better to serve the needs of the Confederacy," the sergeant said, roughly pulling her out of the way.

She remained in his grip while the gate was opened. After the horses had been roped and led outside the sergeant pushed her aside. "Now for the rest of the livestock."

★ ★ ★

It was an hour later. The unit was clear of the Connors' spread and making its way east, nearing base camp. Sergeant Henderson was pleased with himself. He had been ordered to bring in supplies and would arrive in camp with three cows, a dozen prime horses and a wagon stacked with freshly slaughtered hog meat. That would stand him in good stead with the major.

"It just occurs to me," he said to the man riding alongside him. "That place we've come from. Belongs to a guy who refused to join the ranks."

"Yeah?"

"Yeah. We paid him a recruiting visit a spell back. I remember him. Mean bastard. Figure he needs to be learned a lesson."

"Reckon he's already had his lesson, Sarge, losing his hosses and stock."

Henderson chuckled. "This bozo deserves another lesson — and we can have some fun into the bargain."

* * *

Tom Connor was feeling good. He'd sold two horses and got a good price. As he rode, his mind turned to the nursery he was kitting out. When he had concluded his trading he'd dropped in town. He hadn't stayed long, wishing to get back to Mary, but long enough to see a crib in a store and put a deposit on it. The next time he came to town with a wagon he would bring it as a surprise for the mother-to-be.

But all these thoughts disappeared when he got in sight of home — or what was left of it. The main building was a smouldering shell.

"Mary!" he yelled as he threw himself to the ground. He ran to the couple of smoking uprights that had marked the door and he surveyed the charred mess.

He looked across at the corral. The gate was open and the horses gone. He ran round the outbuildings, looking in each and shouting his wife's name.

Inside the barn, he found the still form of the dog. He knelt beside the animal. There was a bullet hole in its skull.

Back at the cabin, he ventured in. He kicked at still-hot wood. Then he found a body. There wasn't much left — but it was Mary.

He stumbled outside and dropped to his knees, overcome with grief.

★ ★ ★

"Mary's dead," Tom said. Grief-stricken, confused, he had not known what to do and had ridden over to the Burgess place where he had found Mary's sister Ruth alone.

Ruth whimpered as he said the words and he just managed to catch her in the doorway as she collapsed. He helped her to the sofa where she crumpled in a heap.

"Indians, I think," he mumbled. "But never known 'em to cause trouble before."

It was a long time before she was composed enough to speak and then it was in weak, tear-laden tones. "We knew something bad had happened, but not that bad."

"What do you mean?" he asked.

"Ned saw the smoke on the horizon," she whimpered, "and knew by the direction it had to be your place. He rode over with some of the boys and said it was burnt down but that you and Mary had gone."

"No. I wasn't there but she was. I

found what was left of her under the burnt-out rubble." He couldn't control his crying when he explained how he had buried her. Pulling himself together he managed to say, "Where's Ned?"

"He didn't know what to do. Didn't know where you were. He rode into town looking for you."

"I dropped by town on the way from my trading, but didn't stay long. He must have missed me."

They sat quiet with their thoughts for a spell, then Tom said for sake of something to say, "Suppose the only thing to do for now is wait for Ned to come back."

She made coffee and they sat quietly until they heard hooves outside. Tom stood up and a moment later Ned limped in.

"Dropped everything when I saw the smoke and headed over there," he explained after their first exchanges. "But the place was a fireball. I did what I could with water from your well but it was hopeless. I saw no signs of you and Mary. Figured the two of you were away somewhere. Seeing's there was nothing anybody could do until the fire had followed its course, I came back here, told Ruth and then went to town looking for you."

"Ain't no accident," Tom said. "Somebody done this. Found the dog — shot. Ain't no accident, Ned. What you think, renegade Indians?"

Ned pulled emotionally at his beard. "No. And I think I know who. It's all over town."

"What the hell you talking about?"

"Story is there was this soldier getting drunk out of his skull in one of the saloons. Then a couple of army fellers came in looking for him and charged him with desertion."

Tom nodded. "I gathered there'd been some commotion in town but I was eager to get back and didn't stay to ask. What happened?"

"Well, the feller wouldn't go with them and there were words between them. Everybody in the saloon heard it."

"What words?"

"Feller's mind had almost gone with the booze. Starts taking his uniform off saying he couldn't be in no army that did things like what he'd seen."

"Like what?" Tom said impatiently. "What had he seen?"

"Seems he had been on a detail to commandeer supplies for the CSA. Livestock, horses and such. There's something big coming up. Federal forces are on the way from the Red River."

"Yeah, I heard."

"Anyways, they'd gone to your place and taken your stock."

Tom hissed.

"Then they moved on," Ned continued, "and camped some distance away. While they was relaxing a couple of guys broke ranks, sneaked away to return to your place for some funning." He paused, finding difficulty in finding the right words. "From what this guy said they did things to Mary, Tom."

Tom gritted his teeth and closed his eyes. "Go on."

"Well, she put up a struggle. It got out of hand and one of them killed her. They set fire to the place to cover up the evidence. The one getting drunk in the saloon was the weak one of the pair. Said he'd only tagged along for a bit of fun. But he couldn't take what had happened and deserted. Anyways, he refused to go with the soldiers so they took him out and shot him. Right there in the main street outside the saloon."

"The other one," Tom queried, "the ringleader. What's happened to him?"

"Don't know." He thought some then added, "But the deserter referred to him as Henderson."

Tom mulled over the name. "Henderson, Henderson? I've heard that name somewhere. Yes, that was the name of the sidekick of the colonel who came to my place a spell back trying to get me to volunteer. Youngster, with a wart on

106

his face. I remember him. Called me yellow." Underneath the fire-grime his face blanched and his features stiffened. "I'm gonna get that bastard."

"There's troops all over the place. They're mobilizing to meet this Federal force coming across from the Red River. There's not much you can do apart from telling the marshal in town."

"Ned, I'm gonna get that bastard if it's the last thing I do."

Ned tried to hold his arms as he rose. "Don't do anything stupid, Tom. You can't take the army on."

"Wanna bet?"

And he was gone.

9

HE made his way through the landscape of soldiers many in their 'cadet grey'. Some were heaving on heavy artillery, some tending horses, some loading and unloading wagons, others sitting on their knapsacks and bed-rolls. It was noisy. Officers were yelling orders, others shouted to each other as they manoeuvred heavy burdens on to wagons while some seemed to be shouting just for the hell of it.

Tom stopped near a young man stacking old-fashioned smooth-bore muskets. The soldier looked from the weapons to the man who had joined him. "What I wanna know is, how we gonna win a war with old stuff like these muskets?"

Tom commiserated for the show of it and then asked, "Say, pal, where can

I find the commanding officer?"

"That's a funny voice you got, mister. You ain't a Yankee spy, are you?"

Tom felt like snapping back that he wasn't bothered about either side in this damn bloody war, but restrained himself and said, "Och, no, kid. It's a trace of the old Scots you can hear."

The soldier pointed to two flags dominating the scene on raised ground: one the company pennant, the other the Confederate Jack, a field of blue studded with seven stars in the upper left corner and three red and white stripes. "Colonel Boscum is in the big tent yonder, but I doubt if he'll see you."

Tom strode over but the commander's tent was sealed off from access by several rings of sentries.

"Like to see Colonel Boscum," Tom stated to the sentry on the outer ring.

"So would a lotta folks, mister," the soldier said, without moving.

"It's real important."

The man pointed away sharply with his thumb. "Don't bother me, mister."

"What is it?" another voice interjected. Tom turned to see a man with sergeant's markings.

"I would like to see the colonel, sir."

"No chance. What's it all about?"

"It's a matter of justice."

"Justice?" The sergeant guided him to one side by the shoulder. "What do you mean, justice?"

"An officer has killed my wife. It's my figuring the critter's here somewhere."

The man took out a watch from his tunic, checked it, sighed and said, "Very well, tell me more about it."

Tom went through the details.

On the conclusion the sergeant began by saying, "Well I don't know how much truth there is in what you're saying but . . . " But he was interrupted with "I'm no liar, sir."

"Let me finish. Even if there is

something in what you say there's nothing that can be done. The company is gearing up to move out. The Union army is heading in from Louisiana."

Growling, "Let me speak to the colonel," Tom made to push past him but the sergeant indicated to two sentries who had been observing the exchange and they grabbed the civilian.

"Now listen up, farmer," the sergeant said, his voice suddenly hardened. "We've had orders to mobilize and move out as soon as possible. That's a thousand men, their equipment and supplies that need organizing. You think anybody's got time for petty civilian slanders?"

"Petty?" Tom roared.

The soldiers restraining the visitor had to drop their rifles to get a better grip. "Get him off the camp," the officer said. "But keep the horse. We're commandeering that." Then he turned to Tom. "You got any beef with the army, write a letter to General Lee!"

At the periphery of the site he was

111

thrown to the ground. He leapt to his feet, breathing hard. He curbed himself just enough not to hurl himself back at his escort, who stood looking at him, rifles at the ready. Under their gaze he wandered off and dropped on his backside under a tree.

No place to go back to. Now no horse. Ned was right. You can't take the army on. Even if he did put in an official complaint, the grey-bellies would cover each other. The town marshal would have no better leverage than himself, like a flea on a buffalo. And who in the army bureaucracy was going to bother about the killing of one woman when according to the latest news hundreds were already dying, maybe thousands.

Well, Mary's murderer was somewhere in this camp. He was sure of that. A man in uniform by the name of Henderson. Now he was this close, he wasn't turning his back. But how could he get to the bastard?

* * *

It was half an hour later, his breathing had calmed somewhat and he was standing before the recruiting officer.

"Arms and legs, two of each, you'll do," the man said in answer to Tom's offer of enlisting. "Any weapons, a horse?"

"You've already had my horse. What I've got is what you see."

"Not to worry. You might get some kit eventually. Put your name down here."

* * *

The company moved out the next day. Tom took on his new role as private in the Confederate Army and did as he was bid. He had calmed down enough for his brain to operate on a calculating level and he had enough sense not to start asking questions at such an early stage. Somewhere along the column snaking eastwards to meet

113

the Union invaders was a man called Henderson. A young man with a wart on his left cheek.

He wouldn't make his search conspicuous, he wouldn't ask curiosity-arousing questions. He would bide his time, listening, looking. Content that his quarry would not be very far away. He had one aim: to get himself a chance to kill the son-of-a-bitch before the enemy did.

10

ON the march the ranks swelled as units joined, only to contract as corps were redeployed. Regiments were merged, then sections hived off. It was a rag-taggle army with no set pattern to the establishment of fighting groups. With such comings and goings it was difficult to keep track of personnel save for the men in a man's immediate unit.

Each morning bugle calls echoed over the open land and Tom arose to look over a growing horde across the landscape. And each morning he listened carefully to roll-calls, ears straining for the name of a man called Henderson who might have arrived during the hours of darkness.

The Texas Brigade was a rag-taggle army in all senses. Most men, young and old, had never fought. Yet they were signed up and were expected to march in formation. On the move they looked like hicks casually strolling to Saturday market. A man was expected to bring as much of his own kit as possible. There were few uniforms and fewer arms for those who hadn't brought a weapon. Of the latter some received an old-fashioned smoothbore musket from the limited stores.

Despite the Confederacy being outnumbered the morale of the men was not low. They knew theirs was to be a defensive fight. The Union were to be the attackers; the blue-bellies were the ones who would have to go out on a limb on foreign terrain.

Rumours abounded amongst the men but then, as they approached the Louisiana border, came hard intelligence that Banks's force had left the Red River and was headed their way. With the prospect of action, there was a sea-change in the attitude of the men and Tom's mind was forced from his quest to the more immediate task of staying alive.

Tom was issued with a smooth-bore musket and, along with the other greenhorns, was given limited drill and shooting practice each time they bivouacked. They were in Sabine country someone said, but that meant nothing to the Scot. Then practice was stopped and, under orders to remain quiet, they marched in short bursts, stopping more frequently.

The reason was soon apparent when they heard the crackle of real gunfire in the distance. Tom was aware of the apprehension in the eyes of their young officers. Then, cresting a ridge to the increasing sound of distant firing, they saw puffs of smoke on the slopes ahead.

There were discussions between officers and Tom's unit was detailed to move along the ridge and descend some distance away. Part way down they were ordered to fire at the blue specks on the valley floor. The engagement didn't last long. The Federals were in a spot and soon retreated out of sight.

Tom looked down at the now silent bottom of the valley. There were unmoving figures in Union uniforms lying on the ground. Whether Tom's firing had accounted for any he didn't know, and didn't want to know.

★ ★ ★

The ensuing engagements followed the same pattern. It was broken hill country with wagon roads few and little clear space for open battle. Despite the Federals' larger numbers the terrain around the Sabine was unknown to them and Tom found himself alongside his fellows, taking potshots at uncoordinated troop columns.

It is the nature of battle that the man on the ground has no idea of the big picture. All Tom knew was that he fired and advanced when ordered. Then, within a couple of days, whatever had happened was all over. At least for the time being.

They fixed camp and bided their time. Eventually news came that Banks had been beaten and sent reeling. The expeditionary force against Texas was in full retreat.

The first engagement by the Texans had been a victory and Tom celebrated with his comrades.

* * *

From then on times were quiet. There was much drilling and preparation and in between men exchanged anecdotes about their experiences. But everyone had a feeling this was just the beginning. Their first taste of action had been no more than an entrée to the big meal ahead. Again rumours abounded but what was known was that the Union were now starting to come down in two sweeps. One thrust was in the East against the Confederate capital of Richmond. The other in the West which had to be an attempt to gain full control of the Mississippi River and its tributaries.

★ ★ ★

Time passed and Tom gained no clues to the whereabouts of Henderson. As they contemplated renewed contact with the enemy thoughts of his quest were again driven from his mind by the everyday practicalities of soldiering.

In time he saw blue uniforms again, heard weapons fired and pulled the trigger of his old musket when ordered. In his unit there were a few woundings but only one fatality. The only injury Tom received was a kickback from his ancient weapon which embedded a scatteration of black marks in his cheek. The thing was dressed and was sore for a while but soon forgotten. During his brief recuperation he was at last issued with a grey uniform.

From then on, the Texas Brigade were involved in minor engagements around the tributaries of the Tennessee and the Cumberland, but the contacts were nothing more than exchange of fire between small units. Then news came of successful attacks on the northern borders of the Confederacy where Grant had taken Fort Donelson on the Cumberland River and Fort Henry on the Tennessee.

These were major Union victories and hit the morale of the Southerners, necessitating second thoughts among the high command. While strategies were being contemplated news came through that the Union had pressed further south and achieved a major victory at Shiloh.

It was clear that Grant was definitely putting into effect the plan of aiming for control of the Mississippi River and its tributaries. In his way stood Vicksburg, seen by many as the key to the Mississippi.

President Davis recognized its importance, describing it as 'the nail that holds the South's two halves together' and Tom's unit was one of many ordered across the river to help defend the city in case of attack.

The Confederate garrison at Vicksburg were hopeful. It was a well-fortified stronghold that had already easily repelled attempts at capture. The men became even more complacent when Grant's advancing army seemed to disappear from the map. Wherever the enemy soldiers were, they would be tired, having been forced to hack its way through forest and swamp, and had abandoned its lines of supply.

There was no perceived threat.

For a while things were calm. But the Southerners' intelligence had been deficient. What they didn't know was that Grant had steamed down the river and disembarked on to the western bank. He had then organized supplies and a means of crossing the river using Union ships which had succeeded in getting south of Vicksburg.

After a short siege the city fell from a surprise attack from the east.

Tom along with all surviving Confederate troops was taken prisoner. The two armies were still following a policy of prisoner exchange and after a short spell in a camp close to the fallen city, Tom was freed to head west.

★ ★ ★

Unconquered Texas was still in a position of strength. The prosperity of what some called Kirby-Smithdom was an embarrassment to the administration who were aware of the privations of the Confederacy east of the Mississippi. General Kirby Smith repeatedly tried to get supplies through but the Federals guarded the great waterway at strategic points. However, the river stretched for such a distance that there were holes in the Union defences and small convoys of supplies made it through.

Tom was not interested in any of this until he heard that among the last small wagon train to leave there had been a Sergeant Henderson. It was the first time he had heard the hated name since he had joined the ranks of the grey.

He volunteered for the next convoy and soon found himself crossing the Mississippi under a Captain Beauchamp of the Army of Virginia. The officer was young, inexperienced and indecisive. However, the small unit didn't run into any of the enemy so, despite the leader's inadequacy, they made it to Richmond. They were greeted warmly by the defenders there, but the men of the Texas Brigade realized their contribution was a drop in the ocean in relation to the needs of the beleagured city.

Tom wanted to stay because he felt sure the man he sought was now part of the city garrison but he was ordered back with Beauchamp. They hadn't been on their return journey very long when they ran into heavy Union troop movements coming north. The small unit tried to double back but found their route to Richmond cut off. The

Federals were clearly aiming to encircle the Confederate capital.

Their small unit now virtually surrounded by blue uniforms, Beauchamp wanted to surrender, but his subordinate officers talked him out of it. The only option was to ride north, he'd pointed out, and that was crazy for Confederates. But he was a coward with his officers too, and allowed them to persuade him to give the order to ride towards Northern Virginia.

As they moved into low hill country they came across an isolated Federal unit taking a bivouac. Beauchamp wanted to skirt around them. They were well into Union territory, he had argued. There was little a small Confederate unit could do. Again his men prevailed. Better to capture a few Federals than do nothing.

They duly encircled the camp and gave verbal challenge. A few shots were exchanged, one Union man was killed and a couple injured, before the unit surrendered. Somewhere to the east heavy Federal forces were moving down on Richmond and the small unit had been sent out to gather supplies from the land. But this was Virginia where farmfolk supported the Rebel cause and were prepared to burn consumables rather than let them fall into northern hands, so the small group had had little success.

Beauchamp became a 'brave' man again and wanted to shoot the prisoners, but once more his men persuaded him to take another course of action. They agreed with him that, given they were virtually surrounded by northern forces, there was little they could do militarily. However, their argument ran, they could help to keep some Federals out of action by taking them prisoner for the duration. And there should be no problem in finding local Virginians to give them succour in their task.

11

IT was early April, 1865. The place was Julesville, a small town in Virginia, and Captain Beauchamp was in an embarrassing position.

The Rebels had taken away their enemies' weapons and marched their captives to the nearby Julesville. The local doctor was prepared to supply his services to the few wounded and the town council were agreeable to the incarceration of the remainder in the school-house. But captors and captives were war-weary and the relationship between them, at first formal yet respectful, soon became casual to the point of open friendliness. The captured Federals were allowed freedom in and around the school-house on their word that they wouldn't try to escape. The two sides shared food, tobacco and conversation.

The reason for the Confederates' embarrassment over their advantage was because both sides knew the writing was on the wall for the South. Although the town was isolated, news was coming in. The CSA had lost all major engagements since early '64 and since the previous fall most rational-thinking Southerners had realized the technical conclusion of the war was only a matter of time. Whether or not President Davis was a rational man he was certainly resolute, determined to see the conflict through to the end, no matter how bitter. As long as Richmond survived, the cause endured. In fact the scuttlebutt was he wouldn't even acknowledge that as the end. It was said he had drawn up contingency plans for survivors to take to the hills and prosecute guerilla warfare.

Over the days news filtered through piecemeal to the isolated unit at Julesville. Things weren't looking too good in Richmond, the Army of North Virginia was closing fast on the capital.

Given the indecisiveness and general incompetence of the small unit's captain it was a marvel the company had been successful in their last action. Tom and the other men knew why. It was because their leader, schooled in leading from the rear, was carried by those under him. The brief action over, it had been they who had explained to him the virtue in sitting tight and waiting on developments from the last theatre of war. And it had been they who had managed to persuade him to treat their captives like human beings in the interim.

Cocooned from the bloody conflict to the south, the men of both sides filled their time with various activities: throwing horseshoes, playing cards and the like. Tom had discovered that one of the Northerners, a young reticent trooper by the name of Joe, could play chess and the two of them had developed a friendly rivalry.

One afternoon the men had finished a meal, eaten outside under the warm spring sun. The food was supplied by the townsfolk. Until the recent action between the two units who were now in a way their guests, the town had been largely unaffected by the war and the folk had carried on their normal life working the land. As a consequence the fare was wholesome and there was plenty of it.

By now all barriers had broken down between the two groups of differently uniformed men and Tom had taken his meal as usual in the company of the young Joe. They were sharing a smoke afterwards when the youngster said, "You know, Tom, you ain't a bad guy — for a Reb."

Tom chuckled. "I ain't really a Reb. Not a dyed-in-the-wool one, anyways."

"Then you don't believe in the Rebel cause?"

The lad was talking more than he usually did. That was a good sign for Tom had observed that the sparkle of youth was missing from his eyes, as it was for many of the young men in battle-marked uniforms. Any length of time at war was a long time.

"Shouldn't be talking like this to one of the enemy," Tom said, "but, fact is, issues ain't clear-cut. There's arguments on both sides. Even old Sam Houston was against secession at the start. Did his damnedest to keep Texas out."

"I didn't know that."

"Yeah. That's why Texas came in on the tail-end."

"Then how come you enlisted?"

"Got kinda mixed up with the thing, like a lotta men, I suppose." He refrained from going into detail. "Just a matter of time and place. Hell, I'm beginning to forget the reason why I put the grey uniform on in the first place. Don't tell my captain but it makes no never-mind to me who wins."

"That explains something. I been listening to your voice while we've been having our talks these past few

131

days. There's Texas in it, but you ain't Texas bred, are you?"

"No. Hail from a place a lot damper."

"Further north?"

"Further east. A helluva lot further east. Bonnie Scotland."

The youngster slapped his thigh. "Hell's teeth! My grandpappy was Scotch!"

Tom nodded. "Small world."

"Ain't it so?" The youngster shook his head as though in disbelief, then took a photograph from his pocket and handed it to Tom. "That's my girl. Molly."

For a moment there was sickness in Tom's heart as he looked over the picture of another man's girl and remembered his Mary. Some guys were lucky to have someone to go back to. "Sure is a looker," he said. "Must be aching to get back to her."

The young one took it back and gazed at it. "Listen, I feel I can trust you, Tom. You do me a favour?"

"Depends. Remember, you're supposed to be my prisoner and I'm supposed to be a guard."

The young man took some documents from his pocket. "These letters. I've written 'em for Molly but ain't had no chance to mail 'em. If anything happens to me, will you send them on? The address is there." He took out a fold of Union bills. "Some money too. She'll be needing that if I don't make it back."

Tom laughed. "Nothing's going to happen to you. You're out of the shebang now. Figure I am too, the way events are turning."

In the circumstances it might have seemed odd for the lad to express such fears. He was being treated well, food was in good supply and there was no threat to him here in Julesville. But the lad was edgy and Tom had noted how he would occasionally roll his eyes and hug himself. He recognized the symptoms, he'd seen them often in the last year. It was the way war got to some men, young or old. Losing buddies, seeing things that no one should see.

"Don't fret, kid," he said. "You'll be home soon."

But the lad was insistent about his request. "I'd be obliged, Tom."

The other took the letters and pushed them into his tunic pocket. "OK," he said, slipping the bill-fold into his back pocket. "If it'll keep the peace between us."

★ ★ ★

The next day a couple of haggard Confederate infantrymen staggered into Julesville. Men of both sides gathered round them as they reported on the situation they'd left behind. Lee had pronounced Richmond no longer tenable. Davis and his government had left by train for Danville. Food riots had broken out in the Confederate capital; there was looting and the place was being put to the torch.

Then Lee had left, heading south hoping to outdistance the Federals and join Johnston for a last stand. But the ragged army was being cut off on all sides. Men were being captured or simply going home. The two foot-soldiers who had made it north to Julesville reckoned that when they had quit, the force of 60,000 that had set out from Richmond was down to less than half and reducing fast.

Captain Beauchamp listened to their tale then, despite the protests of his officers, put them under arrest pending court martial for desertion. That night the two men mysteriously escaped.

He was fuming next morning. Said the place was too lax and if he found out which of his men had turned a blind eye to the defectors' escape he would see they faced a court martial.

But his posturing was of no consequence. Three days later a steady stream of men in blue and grey started to pass through the town. *Everybody* was going home. Lee and his Army of North Virginia had surrendered at a place called Appomattox. It was all over.

There was nothing Beauchamp could do. His prisoners shook hands with their captors, retrieved their weapons from the stack and walked off. Then the men of his command began to drift away before his eyes.

* * *

Tom didn't leave immediately for a couple of reasons. Firstly, he wasn't sure of his own future and he hadn't had the luxury of time alone to think about it. He envied the men who were heading home. One thing he knew, there was nothing left for him in Texas. And the war had taken precedence over his search for Henderson. What did he know about his whereabouts? The man could be anywhere; by now the critter might even have been killed in action.

Save for the wounded the only combatants left in town besides himself were the captain, who was as indecisive as ever, and his young Union friend Joe Hall, who gave the appearance of a lost soul. And that was the second reason Tom hadn't lighted a shuck like the rest. He'd taken a shine to Joe and wanted to see he was all right and headed squarely back to his Molly.

"There's really nothing left to do, Ed," Tom said after they had washed and shaved one morning. It was the first time he had called Captain Edmund Beauchamp by his first name. "Save for making a final check on the wounded. They're in capable hands and we know the folk hereabouts will see them right."

"Suppose you're right. But it's just taking time for it to sink in that we're at peace. That the whole thing is over."

Tom realized the significance that the last statement would have for his former superior officer. In the short time he'd been under his command he'd recognized the type: an incompetent who would be lost in a world without regulations. But understanding the poor guy's problem, that he had little inside him, didn't mean he liked him.

He looked at Joe, saw another of life's casualties, and figured he'd have to make his decision for him. "Well, me and Joe are heading north, ain't we, Joe?"

The former Federal trooper nodded. "Reckon so."

Tom looked back at the captain. "Where's your home town?"

"North Virginia," Beauchamp said. "Near the border."

Tom nodded. "You're welcome to keep us company on the way." He didn't mean it but it seemed the thing to say.

12

IN less than an hour they were ready to march. They had made a final check of the wounded but they already knew that each was well on the way to recovery. Joe was allowed the return of a rifle. They were given biscuits and hardtack by the townsfolk. Captain Beauchamp touched his cap in a military salute to the town officials and the gathering of folk who had come to see them off and the trio set their feet towards the north.

It wasn't long before they came across a homestead and the folk came out to ask for news. They passed on what they knew before continuing. Every so often they would come to another dwelling or small settlement and each time they would repeat the information.

As they strode on Tom kept an eye

on Joe, looking for signs that his frame of mind was improving. He didn't cotton to walking the kid the whole way back to the Potomac or wherever the youngster lived; but he reckoned if he walked some way it might help to unwind the kid. He'd seen some men, men with the same look Joe had, break down and cry when left alone.

That evening they bivouacked in a barn courtesy of a farming family, then headed out again early next morning.

With the three of them well into the routine of journeying, Tom pondered increasingly on his own future. More and more he moved to the conclusion that he would head back to Texas. If Henderson was still alive there was a chance that the man would gravitate back to his home state like the rest of the veterans. Tom knew it would be like looking for a needle in a haystack, but his life was sorely in need of some purpose and the resumption of his search for the wart-faced son-of-bitch would provide it.

The only thing that stopped him turning tail right now was the young Northerner. Tom felt the kind of obligation one might feel to a young pup. It was some hours into the afternoon and they took a break from their foot-slogging, dropping under a tree to rest their aching limbs.

"Hey, listen to the birds," Joe said after a while. He was lying on his back, arms crooked under his head, a piece of grass in his teeth. "Have you guys noticed? They've started singing. You know, it's just like somehow they know the war's over."

"That's a poetic thought," Tom said. "But our feathered friends have always been doing their chirruping. It's just that you ain't had a notion to hear 'em for a long, long spell."

The men became silent again and Tom pondered on the lad's remark. His making the simple observation was a good sign. A man who can revel in bird-song couldn't be all that twisted inside. Ever since news had come through of the cessation of hostilities he'd been aware that Joe had been brightening up. And the improvement had continued as they had covered the miles from Julesville. This seemed to clinch it. Joe was returning to how a kid his age should be. Yeah, Tom wouldn't feel so guilty leaving him now. He could abandon the pup.

"Can I have a look at your map, Ed?" he asked.

The captain passed it over and Tom unfolded it, laying it on the ground. They were approaching the Rappahannock. If he was going to head Texas way he'd already got to backtrack quite a spell and he didn't cotton to having to cross a river twice into the bargain. He moved his finger across the crinkled surface of the chart. If he turned south-west hereabouts he should be able to work his way down along the edge of the Appalachians till he found a break in the foothills with a road heading west. With luck he should be able to hitch a ride.

He made his decision known to the others. The three kicked a few words around, then Tom said, "Could I take the map with me, Ed? It'll sure be useful."

"Certainly. I got no more use for it."

They rose and stood silent for a few seconds, all three conscious of the awkwardness of the moment.

"You've been a good soldier, Tom," the captain said. Tom felt like saying 'What the hell do you know about good soldiering?' but it wasn't the time to voice such thoughts.

"Been an honour to serve under you, Captain." He didn't mean that either.

"Gonna miss you, Tom," Joe said. "Real appreciated your company back there in Julesville."

"You marry that Molly and get started on a family pronto," Tom said. He shook hands with each of them and hoisted his warbag on his back. With their wishes for a safe journey back to Texas he set off, throwing them a last wave before he disappeared over a rise.

★ ★ ★

It was some time in the afternoon when the two young men crested the top of a ridge. They stood for a moment surveying the valley before them. It was green, quiet, untouched by war. They breathed deep of the clean air and began to descend heavy-footed through the long grass. There was a stand of trees at the bottom and they dropped to the ground under the branches of the first one they came to.

Captain Beauchamp examined the soles of his boots. They were wearing thin. "I can feel every pebble I tread on. Hungry too." He opened his bag. "Fed up of biscuits and hardtack."

"Figure I saw some jack-rabbits as we came down the grade," Joe said.

The officer patted the pistol in his standard-issue holster. "I've only got this. Ain't the best weapon for hunting."

Joe picked up his rifle. "Pay no never-mind. I used to hunt a mite back home. I'll go and see what I can bag. That is if you don't mind fire duty, I mean, you being an officer an' all?"

"Hell, no."

"OK, get some kindling but don't light it till you hear me call. We're downwind all right, but you never can tell with smoke. God's critters seem able to nose it, no matter which way the wind's blowing."

The Southerner began scratching around for kindle while Joe moved some distance along the line of trees. He sat down, his back against a tree-trunk, eyes on the green slope. He cradled the rifle on his knees and became quite still as his pa had taught him.

"Once you're downwind," his pa would say, "the only thing you gotta concentrate on is keeping still. You keep as still as a tree. It's movement the critters see. You don't move and your prey don't know you're there." He slowly raised his rifle then froze.

Meanwhile Captain Edmund Beauchamp stacked wood, humming to himself. He put some stones on either side and cut himself a thin branch which he began smoothing to complete the spit. There was a shot. His heart quickened and he looked up. It had been weeks since he'd heard gunfire. There was a pause, the length of time it takes an experienced soldier to reload, then another and a yell. Could have been a Rebel yell if he hadn't known it was coming out of a Yankee mouth.

The fire was crackling by the time the private returned triumphant, his rifle horizontal across his shoulders, his hands coming over the ends, a jack-rabbit in each.

They skinned the animals and sat in silence savouring the smell of cooking meat.

"Your uniform's faded," Beauchamp observed.

"Seen a lotta rain."

"You been wearing it long?"

"Eighteen months or more."

They finally got down to eating and didn't talk much, relishing the fresh meat. Then as they slowed up and picked the bones they talked of their families, their home towns. Joe still found it awkward talking to his companion especially about such personal matters. Although the Southerner wasn't much older than himself, he still saw the man as the one who commanded the unit that had captured his detachment and held them under guard, albeit so loosely.

Then the captain wiped grease from his mouth and asked, "You killed a lotta men?"

Joe wanted to forget such things. They were unsettling, gave him bad dreams. Hell, like Tom said, the damn war was over. And it was sure difficult to talk over such matters with a man who, until a couple of days ago, had been his enemy.

147

"Can't say," he said. He didn't like the specific question. The information it sought he was reluctant to admit even to himself. Then he added, "A few men dropped after I'd sighted 'em and pulled the trigger. You been in action, you know how it is. In the thick of it, I can't say whether it was my ball that put 'em down. Or somebody else's slug. Or whether they was killed or wounded. I ain't one for checking things like that."

There was silence then Joe threw a well-cleaned bone away and went on, "I tell myself they're in some army hospital now and maybe up and walking about." He paused. "That way I can live with myself."

The officer in Beauchamp prompted him to justify the actions. "In war," he said coldly, "you fire because you have to, because you've been ordered. No matter what side you're on."

"I used to see it that way," Joe said. "Joined up when the Union Army came marching through. Flag-waving, drums a-banging. I listened to the big talk. Saw my buddies enlisting. Had to do my bit. You have the uniform on, you're all-fired up and you're feeling proud, excited. Then suddenly, all hell breaks loose. You're in uniform, there's smoke and noise. You got a gun in your hands and you realize you're trying to kill fellow human beings, fellow Americans. That stuff about following orders, that's an excuse. It was *me* that volunteered. I didn't have to. And I know it was me pulling the trigger."

Joe's voice was low and the words came slow. In all his conversations with Tom they never talked about those things. He liked Tom, he seemed to understand. And he didn't like talking about such things now. That's why he didn't ask Edmund how many he'd killed.

Truth was, Captain Edmund Beauchamp didn't know what he would have said if Joe had asked him how many men he'd killed. Probably would have lied. Fact was, he'd killed nobody. But he was an officer, a Confederate officer, from a strong military family. Could he admit he had been to war and not been bloodied? He didn't know.

"Feel like making tracks, Yank?"

"Yeah. Every step's a step nearer home."

13

THE afternoon sun was still hot when they topped a rise and saw a pool before them. It looked cool and inviting. With a 'Yippee' Joe ran down the slope. At the water's edge he shucked his kit and started taking off his clothes. The other watched him until he was in the water before deciding to join him.

Discarded blues and greys lay in crumpled piles side by side. Two young men, neither yet twenty years of age, yet old before their time, regained some of their youth as they splashed and laughed. Then, refreshed they hauled themselves on to the bank.

When Joe was clothed and lying on the bank pleasantly exhausted he watched the other pulling on his uniform. "You got captain's markings," he said. "I figure we're close in years.

You must have been a good soldier to earn your promotion at your age."

Ed shook his head as he buckled his belt. "No, it was my pa bought me my commission. Old military family. He was too old himself to join when war broke out. It was up to me to carry on the family tradition, so he kept telling me." He sat beside his former enemy.

Joe crooked his arms and lay, head back on his hands. "My folks ain't got much. Simple farmers. Make a bitty surplus, but the mortgage eats up most of it."

"Oh, don't get the idea my family's rich. Reckon Pa had to scrape the bottom of the barrel to get the money to swing my commission. But he got it together. Family honour comes first. Huh, couldn't even afford a horse. God, that was humiliating. The only officer in the regiment without his own mount."

Joe didn't understand such things. In the ranks everybody was equal, that's all there was to it. He sucked on a piece of grass. "You married, Ed?"

"No."

"Got a girl?"

"In a way yes. In a way no."

"I don't get your meaning."

"There's a family lives on a neighbouring estate. Their daughter and me, the two families have kinda pushed us together since we were young. Taken it for granted we'll wed."

"What's the matter? Don't you like the girl?"

"It's the other way round. She's always talking about other fellows. How handsome they look in their uniforms. Then, when reports came home, she'd be all fired up about how daring their exploits were in the field. Seems she was always taking the opportunity to ridicule me."

"I'm sorry, Ed."

"Yeah. She kept talking about boys coming back with medals. Don't think I measure up to what she wants." He lay back and closed his eyes. "You got a girl, haven't you? I heard Corporal Connor say something about a certain Miss Molly when we parted company."

"Yeah. We got engaged on my last furlough. She's a real beauty. I been thinking a lot about her. Can't believe she still loves me. We're gonna start our own homestead when I get back. We ain't got much by way of money, but we'll manage. I know it's a corny saying, but I really believe love conquers all." He sighed as he thought about it. "I figure if a guy's got that, nothing else matters."

He suddenly realized that he was stressing his own happiness to a man who was patently without it. He felt guilty and stood up, seeking to change the subject. "Well, the Rappahannock shouldn't be too far ahead. We'll have to go our separate ways from then on."

"Sure is. But we can keep each other company till then."

They picked up their kit and resumed their journey. Their pace slowed with the miles. They talked of childhoods: blissful, innocent summers, schooldays. Like vets they talked of army coffee, sparse mouldy rations, fallen comrades.

Suddenly the river was there, lazing its centuries-old way under basswood trees, unaffected by the wars of men.

"This is it, Yank," Ed said.

They stood on a sandy bar, studying the currents. Both had experienced many partings, but such times still came awkward, and the two young men were ungainly in their handshaking. Joe began to walk slowly backwards upstream, still looking at his companion. He raised a hand in a gesture of farewell to the still unmoving Southerner.

He'd only gone a few paces when he turned. "Hey, Reb," he shouted and retraced his steps. He stopped short. "Catch!" He threw his rifle which the other caught in both hands.

"Don't need that no more," Joe explained. "I meet the turnpike in a couple of miles. There be folks along there who'll be happy to give a returning vet a bite to eat." He pointed downstream. "Looks uninhabited the way you're headed. You might be able to get yourself another jack-rabbit with it." With that he waved a last time, turned and headed north, his knapsack dangling at his side.

The Confederate watched him. He thought of his own impending home-coming. The questions.

Then he checked the musket was loaded. He raised it and fired.

Joe took the ball between the shoulder-blades. He spun round, face incredulous, moving vainly trying to form a question, then crumpled in the moist sand.

The other watched him until he was sure there was no movement, then hurled the rifle into the river.

Now Captain Edmund Beauchamp returning from duty with the CSA could hold his head high during the final miles of his march back home.

Now he could truthfully claim he'd shot himself a Yankee.

★ ★ ★

Tom Connor had been walking for a few hours when he saw the smoke of a camp-fire. Reaching it he discovered a handful of mounted soldiers with the markings of the Army of Tennessee. They were warm in their welcoming, inviting him to join them in their eating. And he was more than happy to see them: not only were they going his way but they had spare horses. At least he could get his rear-end in a saddle.

They were just preparing to move out and he was going through his pockets in search of something when he came across Joe's documents. They didn't amount to much in volume, a handful of unposted letters, but he knew they would mean something to the young soldier. Then there was the money the youngster had entrusted to him.

He stood looking at the bundle while those around him began mounting up, and considered how best to deal with the matter. He could parcel them up, he mused, and mail them when he came to a posting station on his way back to the Lone Star State. But it was chancy. The communications system would still be in disarray following the war. Even in reliable times it wasn't the wisest thing to send money that way.

He figured he owed it to the lad to get the stuff back personal if he could. Hell, he had no reason to rush home like others. Now he had a horse it wouldn't take him long to double back and catch the Northerner up. He owed the kid that. He explained his dilemma to the captain who had no qualms about letting him have the horse.

★ ★ ★

Daylight still held as he approached the Rappahannock River. He dismounted at the edge and looked up and downstream looking for a bridge.

He couldn't see one but reckoned Joe would have crossed somewhere to the north. He hauled himself into the saddle and headed the horse in that direction. He hadn't ridden far when he saw what looked like driftwood near the edge. Up close he could see that it was the twisted shape of a fallen man.

He felt obliged to investigate. Although he had seen many dead men over the last few years he developed a strange unease as he approached the figure. He knew why as he dropped from the saddle. It was Joe. Snipered in the back. He checked in vain for vital signs.

He reasoned Joe and the captain must have separated some ways back to go their different ways, and someone had picked off the young soldier when he was alone. He was old-headed enough to know that this kind of thing happened. No point in looking for perpetrators. But why Joe, for God's sake?

He pulled the sorry figure away from

the river and sat beside his still friend. Familiar guilt feelings rose. Hell, if he hadn't left the young kid this might not have happened. Ambushers would have been less likely to take on two armed soldiers. But what had been the purpose of the attack? The kid's knapsack was untouched. The rifle was gone. He supposed the attack had been simply for the Northerner's weapon.

He looked skyward for a moment. Seems like he'd been the kiss of death to anyone he got close to in this wretched country.

He pulled his mind towards more practical questions and stood up. He looked around. No habitation in sight. He couldn't bury the poor lad here. Where exactly did the kid hail from? He took the letters from his pocket and checked the address. Kingchester, near the Potomac. He took out the captain's map and soon found the place. Still some distance but within feasible range beyond the river. He saw nothing for it but to take Joe back to his folks.

His heart low, he eased the body over the saddle and began the sad journey.

14

THE next day the body began to smell. He was in wooded country and there was some distance yet to go. He couldn't return the lad to his folks in that condition. There was no avoiding it: he would have to see to Joe's last rites himself. Judas Priest, that would be the third person he'd buried in the soil of this damn country.

He was ruminating on these things when a couple of farmers rode up. They paused to give him greeting and he explained his circumstances. If he aimed to bury the fellow, they observed, there was a settlement a short ride ahead. His grim task would be better carried out there, if he had a mind.

He accompanied them to the habitation and was introduced to folk there. The village was too small to have an undertaker proper but it was a self-sufficient place and there was an old woman there who concerned herself with the laying out of bodies for the community. The folk were understanding of his situation. While Tom was fed and given facilities to wash off his trail grime, the old lady cleaned up Joe and did the necessaries, while a joiner set to work with saw and boxplane.

At sun-up the following day he set out for Kingchester aboard a wagon they had let him have, with Joe decently accommodated in a coffin on the back.

* * *

Kingchester was a small colonial-style settlement beside the railroad. Delivering Joe to his parents was a wretched task but something he had to do. He told them his story, explained the circumstances how he had met their son, and explained the good times the two men had had during their short time together.

Once past their initial grief, they questioned Tom about the son they had not seen for a year. The couple were grateful for what Tom had done and took some reassurance in the knowledge that Joe's last few weeks had been spent with a friend.

The burial was quickly arranged and held the next day in the small cemetery a stone's throw from the railroad tracks. At the grave stood Joe's parents in homespun black. Close by stood Molly, other relatives and friends, and a scattering of blue uniforms. During the ceremony Tom stood in his field-grey a decent distance behind the close mourners. He listened to the words of the prayers, the kind of words he had heard so much over the last year.

The folks around the grave were oblivious of a long train that had eased itself to a halt within sight of the cemetery during the ceremony.

While the engineer pursued his task of taking water from the tower, a tall, bearded man dressed in black stepped from a car. He was accompanied by a couple of men who stood at a distance while he took to walking slowly to and fro, clearly taking advantage of the stop to stretch his limbs. As he did so, he looked over his surroundings. His eyes travelled over the settlement eventually coming to rest on the tableau of figures around the grave. Something interested him. After a while he indicated for his companions to join him. The tall man spoke and pointed in the direction of the cemetery. The men listened, raised hands in acknowledgement, then walked towards the group as the tall man returned to the car.

After the 'amen' Tom waited until the mourners began to move away from the grave and presented himself once more to Joe's parents to make his farewells. They invited him to stay over but accepted that he was now eager to start the long trek back to Texas.

He started to make his way to where his horse was stabled when he was intercepted by a man in a suit. "Excuse me, sir. I am a presidential aide. The President would like your company."

"The President?" Tom queried. "President Lincoln?"

"Yes, sir." The man nodded to the train. "In the presidential car."

"President Lincoln, here in Kingchester?"

"If you can hurry, sir. The President is waiting. We do have a schedule to meet."

Tom shrugged, his brain numb. "Lead the way." Puzzled, he followed the man to the railroad. They reached a long car bearing a gilded eagle emblem and the man asked him to wait by the side while he continued along the track to the entrance. Tom could see that another man had fetched Joe's parents and they were now mounting the steps of the car. What was going on?

After a short while the presidential aide who had initially spoken to

166

him returned and called him to the doorway. The man relieved the soldier of his revolver and indicated for him to enter. Taking off his hat, Tom mounted the steps and was shown along the central corridor. They stopped at an open door through which Tom saw an extremely tall, bearded man talking to Joe's parents. After a low-spoken conversation there was a shaking of hands and the couple returned to the door. They smiled hesitantly on recognition of Tom and quietly repeated their farewells to him before passing on their way to leave the car.

When Tom looked again through the doorway President Lincoln had seated himself at the window and was looking at the cemetery. He turned and saw the uniformed man. "Come in, soldier. Please, sit down."

Tom moved in. The interior was lined with rich shiny wood but sparsely furnished with a few chairs and a desk. There were several suited men standing about. Tom sat in the indicated chair opposite the great man who then leaned away from the window, hooking his arm over the chair. "What's your name, soldier?"

"Corporal Tom Connor, sir."

"And your unit?"

"Brigade of Texas, sir."

The President beckoned to one of his attendants and spoke softly. The man left the car, closing the door.

"May I call you Tom?" the President went on.

"Of course, sir."

"You'll take coffee with me, Tom?"

"It would be an honour, sir."

The President made a sign and there was movement around the door and a white-jacketed Negro came in with a tray and served the refreshment.

"I have just given my condolences to the bereaved parents," the President went on in a low, sonorous voice. "I have seen many maimed men, seen many dead men, spoken with many bereaved parents like Mr and Mrs

168

Hall. No matter how many, each is a personal tragedy."

He sighed then said, "You mind if I enquire what ideas you have on politics?"

"You'll understand, sir, I didn't vote for you."

The President smiled as he stirred his coffee. "Fair answer, soldier. But I must ask. Have you any strong ideas about political affairs?"

"Not really, sir. Before putting on this uniform I was a simple horse rancher. With regard to the conflict I didna have any strong feelings either way. For some soldiers, like me, which side you find yourself on depends on geography."

"Is it that you are being diplomatic in the company of a man who, until a few days ago, was your enemy?"

"Ach, no, sir. I'm a plain-speaking man. I wouldna know how to be diplomatic if I wanted to."

"Ach, no," the President echoed. "I've heard that manner of speech back in Springfield, Illinois. Amongst Scotch settlers there."

"Mebbe you have, sir. There's a few of us crossed the water. All like me, come to start a new life, not make war."

"Your origins would suggest that you are truthful when you say you have some neutrality with regard to American rifts."

It was a statement rather than a question so Tom made no reply.

"Well, Tom," the other continued, "I have recently left Richmond, capital of the former Confederacy. The sorry state in which I saw the city is representative of many parts of our country. Now that the conflict is at an end a daunting task lies before us. We need to heal our country's wounds. I see as imperative the need to urge conciliation of the vanquished."

He looked back at the cemetery. "We are on our way back to Washington. The train stopped here for water and I saw the sad ceremony being conducted out there. I was intrigued at the sight of a grey uniform amongst the blue. Your grey uniform. I have spoken to Private Hall's parents but, obviously, in the circumstances it would have been inconsiderate for me to question them too much. Would you like to tell me more about the circumstances?"

Tom related his story, about Julesville, how he had befriended Joe, what had happened and how he had come to Kingchester.

The President absorbed the information. "You see, Tom," he said when the soldier had finished. "I want to see more of the blue and grey coming together. Indeed, for men to forget the colour of their uniforms if they can. As an indication of my feelings with regard to reconciliation I intend to have former Confederates in my administration."

Before he could continue, the man to whom he had earlier spoken returned and gave the President a sheet of paper. The leader perused it. "I took the liberty of telegraphing for any information on you. Of course, in such a short time I was lucky to get anything at all but from the little my staff have managed to discover I see that you have performed creditably for your brigade." He lowered the paper and looked at Tom. "My intention to integrate former Confederates extends to my immediate staff. The brief information on your army record that I have here is enough to show that you have admirable qualities. Furthermore, your actions with regard to a Northerner soldier show that you have a compassion that crosses sides. Corporal Connor, I am inviting you to be a member of my personal staff. Would you be of a mind to accept?"

The thing was moving too fast for Tom. "This is quite unexpected, sir. I don't know what to say."

The President laughed. "You can say 'Yes'!"

Tom's mind raced. He knew that the chance of his locating the killer of his wife now was negligible. If he faced facts it was indistinguishable from zero. Well, he wanted a purpose in life, didn't he? This could be it. An aide to the President of the United States! What would his crofter ma have said about that?

The President checked a watch in his vest pocket. "Well, Corporal?"

"It would be an honour, sir."

15

REACHING Washington Tom was quartered in the White House. There was a couple of days leeway before he formally took up his duties, and in the meantime it had been arranged for a tailor to measure him for a suit. He was in his quarters, holding up his arms with a tape measure around his chest, when there was a knock at the door and a man entered. It was Charles P. Hardie, the President's chief aide.

"Getting settled in, Tom?" the man asked, dropping into a chair and watching the tailor go about his business.

"Sure. But, must admit, this whole thing is a new world for me. The way folk talk, the way they eat. I'm having to learn about things I never even knew about."

Hardie smiled and shrugged.

"Ach," Tom went on, as the tailor lowered his tape measure to Tom's waist. "Even having a suit made to fit my body! I'm not sure I'm going to fit in, Mr Hardie."

"Don't concern yourself with such worries. You won't be the first to feel a little out of place on Capitol Hill. Just remember if you do feel out of place, you're the choice of the President himself. Not many of those who might look down on you can say that."

For a moment the visitor continued watching the tailor going about his activities then said, "Would you mind leaving us a moment?"

"Certainly, sir," the artisan said. He gathered up the tools of his trade and left the room.

"As you have been personally appointed by the President," Hardie said, after the door had closed, "other than the oath of allegiance you will not be given the official briefing normally given to servants of the administration. Your title is that of 'messenger' as the President describes it and your duties will be as he tells you directly. You answer to no one else."

"That's how I understand it," Tom said.

"Fine. But, as with most things in the world, there's more to it than that. For a start, you'll have to understand how the system works here. Now, the President has made the point that he does not wish personal protection. He is quite aware that he is the target of animosity but he feels so strongly about the reconciliation business that he has refused to have bodyguards. His argument is that if anyone is set on assassination, they will do it no matter how many bodyguards are around him. That makes things a little difficult for me. I've taken issue with him on the question but he is adamant so, officially, the matter is closed. Now, as leading aide, I see myself as being responsible for the President's safety whether he likes it or not."

Tom nodded. "I can see your problem, Mr Hardie."

"I'm glad you do. Now the point is, you are one of the few messengers who are going to be close to him, so that puts you in a very special position. As a consequence I'd like you to be armed."

"No problem," Tom said, opening the drawer of his desk and taking out his holstered army revolver.

"Too obtrusive. The President would see the weapon immediately and insist you discard it. Remember, he doesn't want bodyguards. No. You'll need something less obvious such as a shoulder holster. And a slim weapon that doesn't bulge your jacket too much. I'll give you a note. You can get fitted at the military armoury down the block."

Tom nodded and returned his trusty weapon to the drawer.

"One last thing," Hardie said as he headed for the door, "and not the least important. You have been placed in a very delicate position. I shouldn't have to remind you that the bulk of the men that make up the administration here in Washington are Union men. For that reason many of them are against Lincoln taking former Rebels on board. There are senators over on Capitol Hill who've spoken openly against his policy of universal conciliation. So many eyes are going to be on you as a Confederate, looking for a chance to charge you with hanging on to Rebel principles. You've not only got to be clean, you've got to be seen to be clean. They'll be seeking anything which can be construed as your not having full loyalty to the Office of the President."

"I realize that, Mr Hardie."

"Even so, be wary. I'm not talking about treasonable acts. They'll be on the lookout for the slightest sign they can construe that your heart's not in your job."

"I'm not a political animal."

"I think you're an honest john. I've spoken with you and kept my eye on you since you were taken on, and I've got a gut feeling you're on the square."

"Thanks for saying that but you're a dedicated man and I don't think a few days being in my company would be enough to enable you to sleep easy over me."

Hardie chuckled. "You're damn right, soldier. Old Abe is a little more trusting than me. I've had agents check out your whole history. I know as much as records can show about your every step since setting foot on the soil of God's own country. Entering the North-West as an immigrant. Your ordeal at the hands of the Yakima. Then losing your second wife out in Texas. And we've got a pretty full account of your battle record."

Tom dropped his rump on the desk and raised his hands, unable to hide surprise and admiration at the thoroughness. "So much?"

Hardie smiled. "We're talking about

179

the US Government here, Mr Connor. The new telegraph system is a surprising tool." He became serious. "Yes, we know about your losses. You're still a mite younger than me but you've had more suffering than I could contemplate."

Tom nodded.

"But Scot, Texan, American, however you classify yourself now, things are looking up for you."

Tom felt like he'd been stripped bare but felt some warmth in the Chief Aide's last sentiment. "Yeah."

"But remember just as a lot of Southerners are gonna stay unreconstructed, a lot of Union men are going to act like conquerors. Watch your step, soldier. Keep your nose clean."

"Of course."

"Good," Hardie said, rising. As he crossed the room he touched a piece of paper on the desk. "You've seen the programme. You will have read that in a few days time the President is giving a speech outside the White House. Get kitted out with your armoury before then. That occasion will be your first test as a bodyguard."

★ ★ ★

April 11. The President was on the steps of the White House preparing to make a speech. The crowd before him was building up, those at the front being restrained by uniformed policemen. Prior to his address the President was conferring with a secretary of state and a senator.

Tom stood close by, Hardie at his side. "Don't look at the President when he speaks," the chief aide was saying. "There's a natural tendency to do that when you're with him, especially when he speaks. You've been in his company long enough to have noticed there's something magnetic about him. He'll mesmerize you like he does everybody else. Avoid it or you won't be able to do your bodyguarding job properly. You can best do that at times like this by keeping your back to the President as much as possible."

He waved a hand. "Keep your eyes on the crowd, especially their eyes. Be on the lookout for any hint of a crazy expression. Odd movements too. Watch those with their hands hidden, and those who make movements indicating they're going to take something out of a pocket. Don't take your eyes off that person until you're sure whatever they've taken out is harmless. I know it's a lot but on set pieces like this we can divide up the crowd between the messengers so the observation area for each is less. On this occasion you restrict yourself to that section of the crowd."

He chopped the air with his hand, delineating a particular area of the sea of faces. "I've arranged for the other messengers to cover the rest. When I'm otherwise occupied you and the others make your own arrangements about who watches what. When the President is moving around in an unscheduled fashion you'll just have to cope as best you can."

At that point a hush fell on the crowd signifying the President had moved forward. Then Abraham Lincoln raised his hands and began to speak. Quietly, reverentially, Hardie backed away from Tom leaving him to watch the section indicated.

The President proceeded to speak of what he had seen and what the country had been through. Hardie was right. He was mesmeric. From the beginning he held the crowd in the palm of his hand. He spoke of his dreams, his conciliation plans. And there was warmth in his voice as he spoke of Lee and the other Confederate leaders.

Tom watched the listeners, trying to ignore the words. Yes, Hardie was right. Some men, rare men, were different from others. Lincoln was one of them. There was a magic to the politician. The people before him were falling under a spell.

The President continued, pointing to

the paths of goodwill and forgiveness. He spoke of the hard work to come, but a task that would be worth it, paving the way for a bright tomorrow for themselves and their children.

Tom tried to ignore the words. "If universal amnesty is granted to the insurgents," Lincoln boomed in his rich voice, "I cannot see how I can avoid exacting in return universal suffrage, or at least suffrage on the basis of intelligence and military service."

At that point Tom was paying no attention to one of the crowd who turned and whispered to his companion. "Know what that means?" the man muttered. "Nigger citizenship, that's what." It was an insignificant movement and an unheard voice. The man listened to the President a little further and then whispered, "Now, by God, I'll put him through."

Tom didn't hear the man, nor knew who he was.

An out-of-work actor by the name of John Wilkes Booth.

16

14TH APRIL. Tom sat in the corridor outside the President's suite. The President was taking longer over his breakfast than usual. He had his son, Robert, in with him. Captain Robert Lincoln had just returned from the capitulation of Lee and was describing the circumstances to his father.

The attendant heard the door-knob turn and jumped to his feet as someone emerged.

The President was dabbing his lips with a napkin. "Tom. I'm running behind schedule. Pass a message to reception that when Speaker Colfax arrives he is to be directed here, not the office."

"Understood, sir."

The tall man disappeared. His son's visit had been unexpected and Tom was aware that the few hours of the day were already being eaten away. There was a Cabinet meeting at eleven and the President needed to talk over his policy with the Speaker before the meeting. That was usually a long session and the clock down the hall was loudly ticking the minutes away.

When he had relayed the message to the girl at the desk downstairs she asked him to pass on a request to the President. There were some friends from Illinois out front who would like to see him.

"People shouldn't come unannounced and expect him to see them," Tom said, having already developed a natural defensiveness on his master's part. "Anyway, the afternoon's fully booked. There's Governor Oglesby, then Senator Yates. They're all important sessions." In the short time that he had been in the great man's employ he had become aware that he over-worked himself by any normal standard. "This is not some grocery store where you call on a whim."

The girl smiled. Tom's Scots accent rose to the surface when he felt strongly about something. She ensured he didn't see her smile and tapped the paper bearing the presidential insignia on her desk. "I know, Mr Connor. I have the day's programme like everybody else. But these folk have had unexpected business in Washington. They say they're very close friends. I have their names here." She showed him a slip of paper. "Maybe you could show it to him and let me know his reaction? Then I can pass his decision to them."

Tom shrugged and took the paper. He knew his boss rarely turned away folk from his home state. "That's what I'm here for."

★ ★ ★

It was late afternoon. The President had not had time to have a proper lunch. He'd met his commitments and was now talking with the Illinois visitors in the state room. There was a noise at the door to Tom's side. It opened and the visitors came through shaking the President's hand and making their farewells.

"Message, Tom," the tall man said as the party made its way past the marines stationed at attention along the corridor. "This day has been quite a mother. I've still got people to see and Mrs Lincoln and I have had this darn invitation from the manager at Ford's Theatre for tonight's evening performance. Get across to my wife and explain the situation here. Give my regrets but say I'd sure be obliged if we didn't attend." Then he added in a lower voice, "One of those fancy modern plays. If I am going to sit in a draughty playhouse for a night I'd rather it was something classical. You know, edifying. Or, better still, a piece of vaudeville. But don't tell Mrs Lincoln that. Just say I'm running late."

"Yes, sir."

The President returned to his room and Tom set off down the corridor.

In the President's domestic quarters Mrs Lincoln was taking tea with a lady and a uniformed man. The First Lady did not take the news about putting off the theatre visit lightly. "He knows what these things mean to me. Major Roberts is already here and I'll be receiving the rest of our party soon. Dearie me, it's not often we get relief from the demands of the office."

The major tried to explain to his hostess that it would be all right if they didn't attend. To Tom's eyes he didn't look the play-going type either.

"No," Mrs Lincoln said. "It's not often I have my way. And I've been so looking forward to it. Tom, get back to my husband and let him know my feelings on the matter."

With a 'Yes, ma'am', he vacated the room and headed back along the corridor. One thing he didn't like about this job was sometimes having to bounce like a ball between husband and wife. Still it didn't happen too often and it went with the territory.

Back in the room that he had left the major spoke. "Is that man a Confederate?" Tom had picked up enough of a Texan drawl for it to be discernible to those with an ear for accents.

"Yes. It's part of Abraham's policy of reconciliation."

"Yes, I know, ma'am. Your husband speaks about it in his speeches. But, I mean, to have one so close? Is that advisable?"

"Tom is a good man."

"That might be, ma'am, but I've just spent four years fighting Rebs like him."

"Not quite like him, Major. Anyway my husband tells me the man is actually Scotch."

"Begging your pardon, ma'am, but there is a twang in that voice which does not come from Bonnie Scotland. The man's a Southerner, mebbe by adoption, but a Southerner nonetheless."

The First Lady smiled and shook her head. "My husband recognizes a rare compassion in the fellow. Mr Lincoln can do at least two things well: get votes and judge people."

While the President's political skills were unquestioned the major wasn't persuaded on the matter he had broached but remained silent and busied himself with his tea.

★ ★ ★

It was 9.20 that evening when the presidential party entered Ford's Theatre. Lincoln was accompanied by his wife, Major Roberts and three others. Tom spearheaded the group's progress, helping to keep back the crowds in the foyer.

The state box was a double compartment, with separating partition removed, on the second tier at the left of the stage. When the party eventually appeared at the edge of the balustrade the audience rose and clapped.

Tom waited until the cheering had died down and the group were seated then accompanied the departing servants through the small anteroom connecting the box to the corridor.

He closed the door and stationed himself at its side. Alone in the corridor he heard music and then voices. He didn't feel he was missing much. Like the President, he more favoured vaudeville, or music-hall as it was called the one time he had seen it in Glasgow as a child.

It was sometime into the performance when the monotony of Tom's standing alone in the corridor was broken by the approach of a man. He was dark-haired, bore himself with confidence and carried a piece of paper in his hand.

"Yes?" Tom questioned as the man presented himself before the guard.

"I have an invitation to join the President," the man said, his voice having authority if a little bronchial. "Mr Lincoln is expecting me."

"The President didn't tell me."

"Maybe he didn't have time, or forgot to tell you. He extended his gracious invitation just today. Indeed, it is the afterthought nature of the matter which explains my own tardiness." The enunciation of words had formality. Sounded like a politician, somebody used to public speaking. Tom had heard many of them during his service with the administration.

The man offered the paper. "It's been cleared downstairs."

Tom nodded; it would have to have been cleared for the man to have gotten this far. He took the missive and looked it over. He moved a pace nearer the gas lamp to give it further scrutiny. It was an invitation and appeared to be in the President's handwriting as he knew it.

He shook his head. The President's habit of welcoming one and all was an irritation to him. The leader did not want a bodyguard but it had been made plain by Hardie that that was where his duty lay, a duty made difficult by his employer's flexibility. He returned the paper. "Try not to make too much noise," he whispered, putting his hand on the handle. "The performance has started. Particularly, Mrs Lincoln will not take kindly to interruption." He stood aside, opening the door into the darkened ante-room.

"Thank you," the man said and entered.

When the door was closed Tom stretched his arms and resumed his lonely duty. After a while he sought to alleviate the tedium by slowly pacing the corridor. He paused at the end, pulled aside the drape at the window and looked out at the twinkling lights of the capital city. There were many boring times in the job, as at the moment. But it paid well and he enjoyed an opulence of lifestyle beyond the dreams of a Scots crofter's son. And, although not a native American, he felt it an honour to be close to, indeed, serve a man of Lincoln's calibre.

Some men were different; he'd learned that. Lincoln was one of them. Working close to the President, Tom knew him as a human being, knew him as man with foibles. But there was still a quality that he hadn't experienced before. It was difficult to put into words. It had something to do with having a dream about charting the course of a nation and the energy to do something about it.

Tom walked the length of the plush-carpeted corridor and stood at the top of the stairs. One of the theatre staff was at the bottom. Seeing Tom he pulled out his watch, gesturing to it. "Eight minutes to the interval," he said in a loud whisper.

Tom flicked his hand in acknowledgement and turned to resume his post.

But before he reached the door he heard an explosion. He stiffened in his walk. Was it something to do with the play? No, he could hear cries of shock coming from the audience!

He tried the door but, although there was no lock, it wouldn't open. And it was beginning to sound like pandemonium on the other side. He stepped back and crooked his leg. It took two kicks to break the thing open. As he fell into the ante-room, a piece of wood that had been jammed against the back of the door clattered to the floor.

He hurled open the second door and felt the action release a weight. Something slumped at his feet. It was Major Rathbone, his hand round a knife wound in his chest. But worst of all: the President was slumped over the balcony wall, the back of his head a bloody mess. The lady occupants of the box were screaming.

The remaining man in the box, the stepson of Senator Harris of New York, was pointing to the stage. "That's him! That's the one that did it!"

It was the man Tom had admitted to the box, making a limping run across the boards of the stage below. Tom drew the small revolver from his shoulder holster but the man disappeared behind the stage curtains.

He sheathed his gun and bent over the President. He felt for the heart and the wrist pulse. "He's still alive," he yelled. "For God's sake, somebody get a doctor!"

After ensuring the President was in good hands he ran along the corridor, forcing his way through a stream of dazed people.

As he entered the alley at the side of the theatre he took out his gun again. There was a man in a dress-suit standing at the end facing the gas lights of the street.

"He's got away," the man said when Tom joined him.

"Who are you?"

"Stewart. A lawyer here in Washington. I was in the audience." He pointed along the street. "The man rode that way."

"We've gotta inform the police and

military quick," Tom said, more to himself than the lawyer. "See if they can cordon off the city in time." He grabbed the man by the arm. "And you're coming with me, mister."

17

15TH APRIL. The assassin's bullet had entered just behind Lincoln's left ear. Unconscious, the President had been taken to a house opposite the theatre. Tom had been at his side when Hardie had arrived just before midnight. After the aide had had discussions with the doctors he had asked for Tom's account of events.

"Right, Mr Connor," Hardie said when he'd finished, "please return to your quarters and wait for me."

"I'd prefer to stay here at Mr Lincoln's side. I feel bad enough as it is without hanging around in my quarters doing nothing."

"In the circumstances it will be best if you do as I say."

Tom sighed. "You'll let me know how he gets on?"

"You'll be informed."

Tom did as he was bid and it was in his quarters that he learned that the President died at 7.22 that morning. The Scot's world was shattered again, and again by violence. He was churning these things over when Hardie called.

"Mr Lincoln employed you on a personal basis," he said in a formal tone. "Thus you were not part of the official roll. Therefore, with the demise of the President, there is no longer a basis for your services."

"That's it?" Tom queried. "I just pull up my picket pin and leave?"

"Not quite. I'm requesting that you remain confined to quarters pending formal investigation."

"Can't you imagine how sick I feel about this already?" Tom queried. "I understand the need for investigation, but why be confined to quarters?"

"Whether it was official or not, you were Mr Lincoln's bodyguard. And a former Confederate. How do you think that looks here in Washington, Reb?"

The swirling emotions in Tom were compounded with a heavy shot of anger at the suggestion. "What the hell does that mean?"

"It means that for everybody concerned it is best that for the moment you remain put behind closed doors."

★ ★ ★

It was a few hours since Hardie had gone and during that time Tom had been very much aware of the hectic activity in the White House. From his window he could see the many comings and goings. He had friends among the staff and they kept him abreast of developments: Andrew Johnson being sworn in as the new President, the arranging of church services, the planned train ride with the embalmed body of the former leader back to Illinois. But no progress had been made tracing the assassin. After a few more hours of inactivity and brooding he'd had enough.

He slipped unnoticed out of the White House and made his way back to Ford's Theatre. The manager wasn't there. He was trying to pull strings with local politicians to fight the order closing the place. As a businessman he had immediately realized that, as the site of the assassination of the most noted president since Washington, the house would be filled for years to come; but it looked like the administration were going to impose permanent closure.

Tom tracked down one of the caretakers and identified himself.

"Yes," the old man said. "I remember you."

"You saw the murderer?"

"Yes, sir."

"You recognize him?"

"I told the police all I know. Which is little. Like I told them, I got a feeling I might have seen him before, but in this business you see a lotta people. And I only got a glance as he dashed through the wings and out."

Tom thought on it. An idea occurred. "He spoke to me outside the presidential box and he had a very formal voice. At the time he made me think of a politician. But that kind of speaking would also mark an actor, wouldn't it? You say you might have seen him before. This is a theatre. So, an actor, does that prompt anything?"

The old man's face wrinkled further as he kicked the idea around. "You know, young man. I think you're right. I think he might have trod the boards here some years back, now you're pushing me. Mind, if he did, couldn't have been any good because he didn't last long enough for me to remember him too well."

"Can you think of a name?"

The man grunted. "Like I said, I ain't even sure he was here as an actor."

Tom patted the man's arm. "You might have given us a lead here. After

I've gone you must pass your suspicions to the police."

He had acquired some familiarity with the city during his stay and made his way to the Alhambra Theatre a block away. They were putting on some Shakespeare and there was a rehearsal in progress. Tom found the manager in the wings and made himself known as an official without being precise about his status or the reason for his questions. "I'm trying to trace an actor," he said, "and I was wondering if you could help me."

His mind worked over the image of the man that he had seen in the gas-light of the corridor at Ford's. "Shade taller than me. Younger, too. In his mid-twenties. Dark eyes, dark curly hair. Finely moulded features, moustache."

The manager thought about it. "You could be describing any male actor, sir."

"He seemed to have a little trouble breathing," Tom added. "I don't know if the condition was permanent but, if it was, the condition would set him apart from other actors, I would have thought."

"Difficulty in breathing?"

"Yes, he wheezed a little. Had to take obvious breaths in between sentences."

The manager grunted. "That sure would be some handicap for an actor if it was permanent."

"Let's say it was permanent. Any ideas?"

"You know, makes me think of a guy we had in the company here a few years back. Had to dispense with his services because of trouble with his tubes. Couldn't make his voice carry. The more I think of it the more he fits the physical description you give."

"What was his name?"

The man thought. "Booth. That's it. Jim Booth. Bit player, but like 'em all, aspiring to leads. Got quite upset when his condition worsened and he couldn't perform any more. Wouldn't settle for a life as a spear-carrier which is all I could offer him Something of a dark horse too. Nothing you could put your finger on, but wouldn't trust him."

"Know where I can get hold of him?"

"No, not seen him for a year or more. What's this all about?"

"Just a case the administration's looking into to. Well, thanks for your help. You've given me something to think about."

He shook the man's hand and set off through some scenery.

"Wait, mister," the manager called. "It's just occurred to me. I might be able to give something more. Come with me. Let's see what I can dredge up in my office."

The two men went down side steps and walked up the central aisle to the front. Behind them actors were working their way through the text of Hamlet. Someone was talking about there being something rotten in the state of Denmark. Yeah, Tom thought as he followed the man upstairs to a door marked 'Manager', and there could be something rotten in the state of Washington.

"Ain't the most tidy of guys," the man said when they were inside. That was true. There were piles of scripts, rolled up posters and assorted theatrical bric-a-brac all over the place. The man opened a desk drawer and pulled out a jumble of documents. "I keep promising myself I'll go through things in here one day but there's always something more important to do."

He riffled through the mess. "There's more to running a theatre than some folks think. Ain't all glamour and pretty women."

His scrutiny alighted on a letter. "There. An old letter from the very man. See, his full name. James Wilkes Booth. Got an address there too."

Tom looked it over, his heart racing. Fort Royal. If this was the assassin, would he have sought refuge at home? He might do if he was secure in the knowledge that he hadn't been recognized. The whole thing was a long shot, but at least it was something positive, a tangible line he could pursue. He jotted the address down. "You've been very helpful. I can take this letter?"

"Got no use for it."

Tom pocketed it and headed for the door. "The name's Connor. Tom Connor. I'm on the White House staff. Say nothing to anybody about this except if you get a visit from any officials, police, anybody from the administration, particularly the chief aide Charles Hardie or his representative, then you tell them everything about our conversation."

"Sounds important."

"Could be of national importance. That's all I can say. Thank you again for your help."

* * *

Back at the White House Tom found that Hardie wasn't in. He took the letter he had been given by the theatre manager and printed his own name on the top.

"Get that to the Chief Aide," he said to the girl at reception. "He'll know what it means."

In his quarters he packed up his holstered gun and changed into some of his old clothes that he hadn't thrown away. He checked his wallet. At least the job had brought him spending money. In the city he bought a horse and riding gear and, although it was late in the day, mounted up and headed towards Fort Royal.

18

FORT ROYAL was a small settlement on the Rappahannock River. After bivouacking on the journey, he reached it the next morning to find that he was luckier than he had expected. It only took a couple of enquiries to elicit the Booths' household.

The old woman there was Booth's mother. She was clearly agitated and at first denied seeing her son. Although she lived alone there were signs of someone else having been there and under Tom's insistent questioning she admitted to her son's having called.

She was reticent about details but Tom persuaded her it was in her son's interests that she came clean.

"You look a good man," she said. "You won't hurt him?"

"It is not my intention to hurt

anyone, ma'am. But you might have to face that he has committed a crime, a bad crime. If so, he'll have to be punished. No escaping that. It can only be in his interests that you tell me where he is so this thing can be cleared up as soon as possible."

"I knew it would come to this some day," she said. "He always was a headstrong boy. And wanting things his pa and me couldn't give. And all that acting palaver. He lived in a dream world. Then he came in yesterday. Horse all lathered. And him all edgy. Cutting off his hair. I knew something was wrong."

"Where is he now, ma'am."

Her voice fell to a whisper. "He's out at Garrett's farm. It's deserted. Not worked any more." She explained where it was. "Be careful, mister. He's not alone. Please don't push him into doing anything bad. He can have a temper."

"How many's with him?"

"Well, he rode in with one. Dave

Herold. But they got guns."

"Obliged, ma'am. You've done the right thing."

It was a good quarter-hour ride out to the place. There was a farmhouse with collapsed roof, the shells of small outbuildings, the remains of pens and a dilapidated barn. Tom stayed his distance, picketed the horse out of sight and advanced a piece to lie down and watch.

After a spell he was coming to the conclusion there was no one there. The men had ridden on, or the woman had lied. If she had lied, she was good at it because the Scot had believed her.

Well, if the two renegades were there it would have to be the barn; that was the only place that the horses could be kept hidden.

He rose cautiously and advanced. He hadn't proceeded very far when a croaky voice yelled, "Hold it there, mister."

He looked the barn over, couldn't see anybody.

"This might look derelict," the voice went on, "but it's still private property."

Tom could tell the voice was coming from the loading hatch above the swing doors of the barn but he feigned ignorance of its source. "Says who?"

"Never you mind."

"Just looking for a dry place to bunk down," Tom said, moving his head round in pretence that he didn't know where the voice was coming from.

"I ain't telling you again." And a face and gun appeared in the hatch, moving into the sunlight. The last time Tom had seen the face, it had been lighted by flickering gas: without the moustache now and long curly hair shorn to a stubble but, for sure, the same face.

Adrenalin pumped through him. He contained his satisfied surprise and backed to get out of accurate range. "OK, OK."

Reaching a dry horse trough, he dropped behind it. Booth had exposed himself even more and Tom got an even better look at the face, noted the closely cropped head, the Confederate uniform the man now wore.

"Booth," he yelled, all signs of acquiescence now gone from his voice, "I know it's you. I've come to get you. You know what for."

There was a bang and a bullet chipped rotted wood from the trough.

Tom winced, waited, then edged his head enough to have a squint at the hatch. Booth had disappeared but Tom loosed off a shot to let the man know he meant business. Then he heard a different voice coming from the shadow of the hatch. "I told you it would be no good, John. I told you they'd get us."

"Shut up, you yellow belly." It was the bronchial voice of the one-time actor.

"I'm giving myself up."

"There's only one out there. That's one against two!"

There were noises and clatterings, and the barn door inched open.

An unknown face appeared, then a hesitant figure, no guns visible. The man squeezed through the crack, raised his arms and began to advance towards Tom.

When he reached the trough Tom frisked him, then indicated with his rifle for the man to sit behind the wooden stand at the other end.

"I told you there was more than one, Jim," the man yelled as he dropped his backside on to the soil.

Tom was puzzled. Was the man crazy? What the hell was he on about? More than one?

He returned his attention to the barn and was about to resume the exchange with Booth when his eye caught flecks of blue in the distance beyond the barn, half figures shimmering in the heat haze above the long grass of the field. He turned. All points of the compass. They were everywhere, closing in. The man he had just captured had seen them. He lowered his gun and watched a couple of officers break clear.

"Connor?" one queried.

"Yeah."

"You OK? We heard shots."

"Yeah."

"Determined anything positive about the situation?"

"Who are you?"

"Company L of the 16th New York Cavalry, stationed at Fort Royal. Got a telegraph from the Judicial Department in Washington. They gave us your name and Booth's address."

Tom had been wondering how they had managed to follow the matter up so quickly, but he had been forgetting the marvels of the new telegraph system.

"You know my capacity?" he questioned.

"I've been told you can identify the perpetrator."

"Yes. That's the man. In the barn. Booth."

"You certain?"

"I've had a good look at him. I can identify him when necessary. As will about fifty people who were close enough at Ford's Theatre." He pointed to the sitting man. "This guy is some kind of accomplice. Just given himself up. As far as I know there's only the two of them holing up here."

"OK, Mr Connor. Leave it with us now. If you would like to back off and get behind the men there."

"I'd like to see this thing through now I've started it, Captain."

"Well, you can see it through, Mr Connor, but at a safe distance over there. This is now an army matter."

Tom retreated some twenty yards and took cover behind a broken-down wagon. He heard renewed verbal exchanges with Booth but, because of the distance, he couldn't make out words. Then there was silence and a long wait. Maybe they were looking for the opportunity to rush him. Whatever strategy they used they would have to be careful, because Tom was sure they'd be under orders to capture the murderer alive.

Then he saw soldiers, each with

a long object in his hand, circling the building. One by one the men fired brands and hurled them. Most fell against the wall, while a couple of soldiers managed to throw theirs through the hatch. So that was it, they were going to burn him out.

The place being dry and full of straw, it wasn't long before the flames took a grip. Horses whinnied. Cracks in the walls began to light up while smoke and billowing embers rolled out of the hatch.

Above the din there were voices again and the barn door opened. In the wake of the escaping horses a figure emerged. For a moment Tom could see Booth silhouetted against the flames from inside. Coughing, his rifle gone, the failed actor began to walk with raised hands towards the soldiers.

Suddenly there was gunfire. It happened so quickly Tom couldn't tell how many reports. Didn't matter how many because Booth collapsed a few paces from the door. A couple of troopers ran forward bending low, shielding their faces from the inferno that had been revealed by the open doors, and hauled the body clear.

Tom ran forward and pushed his way through the sea of blue. There was blood down the fallen man's grey tunic. His eyes were closed but his lips moved. The words were frog-sounding, there being a gaping, bloody hole in the man's throat. "Tell Mother I died for my country."

The head slumped. If Booth had ever played a death scene, he had just played the best one of his life; and the last.

"You didn't have to order him shot," Tom said to the captain. "Washington would have wanted him alive. History would have wanted him alive."

"I did tell you to keep back, Mr Connor," the officer said.

Tom kept his eyes on the stilled form. "There was no need for that. Not in cold blood."

"He shot the President of the United

States in cold blood, Mr Connor."

"Questions needed to be asked of him. An investigation set up by the Supreme Court. The thing needed to be done in public. So the people of this country know what happened. You're talking like a judge and jury, not a soldier." He paused, then added, "Or were you just obeying orders."

The captain had nothing to say and Tom turned away and looked at his picketed horse. "Well there's no need for me to remain here, that's clear. I'll return to Washington."

"I'd like you to stay in Fort Royal until officials arrive, Mr Connor."

Tom began to walk towards his horse. "No, I'm heading back to make my own report in Washington. We each have our own master."

"In that case, I would like you to accept the offer of a couple of my riders as escort."

Tom grunted. "I'm a grown man, Captain. I rode here alone, I can return alone."

As he rode Tom contemplated what he had witnessed. He had seen it as his duty to seek out the President's assassin. For a short spell he had been figuring that his success in locating the murderer would in some measure help, not only to redeem him in the eyes of Hardie and the administration, but to assuage his own feelings of guilt in letting down his master. But was there was more to this thing than a crazy man killing a president? He felt certain the soldiers had been ordered to kill Booth. But why?

Something else had gnawed at his psyche ever since the night of the shooting. Booth had been seen by a theatre full of people to descend from the President's box, then run across the stage. On his way to the exit he had passed countless stagehands. Yet when Tom got down to the alley, only one man had bothered to pursue him.

And another thing. Booth's horse had stood waiting for him. Why had he been so certain it would be there? And how had Booth been able to make an unhindered getaway on horseback out of the city?

And why had the captain back at Garrett's farm tried to insist on Tom waiting for someone to come from Washington. As far as he knew Tom was an official of the administration. Why did the soldier feel so impelled to make Tom stay?

His thoughts turned from the stream of nagging questions to what waited for him back in Washington. There were signs of trouble there. The animosity towards him as a former Confederate was plain. Hardie had spoken of it as though it was simply a fact to face, but the chief aide's sympathies in that direction had surfaced. With recriminations flying loose he would need support from someone of Hardie's standing but he reckoned he wouldn't get it. Tom was a crofter's son, into something he didn't understand and he felt uneasy.

His discomfort increased manifoldly when, riding through a valley, someone took a shot at him. The first he heard was something whine like a banshee close to his head. Almost imperceptibly later the sound of the rifle report caught up with him from the rear.

His horse started beneath him and, with crouched head, he looked back. There were two riders behind him. Trail bushwhackers or what?

He gigged his horse and sped forward as more shots came his way. Hell, they had repeaters.

He had one thing in his favour: it was dusk. Visibility was lessening fast. Maybe that was why the coyotes had chosen now to make their play.

Despite the fading light the bozos had some luck on their side because he suddenly felt a burn across his outer arm. But luck was with him too: it couldn't be too bad because he could still handle the reins, albeit it with pain.

Ahead he could make out a bend in the trail. That would hide him from the men behind for a while. When he reached the curve he glanced back to ensure he was obscured and turned up the slope into the trees. He gigged the horse and was grateful the animal had enough left in him to make good headway. At the top he dismounted and tethered the horse behind bushes.

From his high altitude there was enough light to give him a view of the trail cutting its way along the valley floor. Through breaks in the trees he could make out the riders. They were uniformed. That bastard captain had sent them. Why?

He watched them come to a straight piece of trail and he could tell by their agitated movements they were disconcerted that they couldn't see him ahead. They exchanged words then spurred their mounts forward. Yes, this was no random bushwhacking.

They had been tailing him. It wasn't just to watch him. He was returning to Washington; if they had been sent by the captain they knew that. No, their objective was more active than mere watching.

Now he had turned he had a lead on them and it would be some time before they realized he had left the trail. Then they wouldn't be sure whether he turned east or west, or at what point.

He examined his wound as best he could in the darkness. His jacket was sticky with blood but his assessment that it was superficial seemed to be confirmed. He mounted up and set off at a pace. It wasn't long before he came to a railroad track. He recognized the terrain. He wasn't far from a little known halt by the name of Kingchester.

19

ONCE he was sure he had avoided pursuit, Tom took his time journeying to Kingchester. It was mid-evening when he drew up outside the Halls' house. They were surprised but glad to see him although disturbed to see his red-sleeved arm. Robbery had become commonplace in recent times, they observed and he allowed them to put that interpretation on his misfortune.

Mrs Hall washed and dressed his wound, then heated leftovers from some stew and he dined heartily.

As he ate they questioned him about his life in the intervening period. Not wanting to involve them or cause them undue concern, he avoided precise details of his short career in Washington. And told them nothing of his suspicions about the attempt on his life. But it was common knowledge he had been taken aboard the President's train following their son's funeral so he got by, inventing some innocuous story about acting in an advisory capacity on the reconstruction programme. According to his tale, his duties in the nation's capital were now over and he was journeying back to Texas.

They talked into the night, commiserated on the death of the President, took a last drink and retired.

* * *

He stayed for a week. Long enough for his wound to be well on the way to recovery. And long enough to have access to a newspaper. Almost the whole issue was devoted to the Washington tragedy and its aftermath. There was no mention of his part in tracing Booth. But there was great deal of debate about the motivation for the killing. The evidence, at least as far as it was presented in the paper, was pointing towards a conspiracy. Over twenty names were given.

It was at that point in his reading that he knew he had to move on. His name was there in black and white, as someone wanted for questioning. Somebody was looking for scapegoats.

Hell, he didn't understand politics. But he did understand that it wouldn't be healthy to return to the capital. Nor healthy for the Hall family if he stayed under their roof much longer.

He made his goodbyes a second time and, loaded with provisions, he headed south-west.

★ ★ ★

As he journeyed he kept in touch with events through newspapers. Someone in the capital was ensuring that the name of Tom Connor stank almost as high as that of John Wilkes Booth himself. Time and time again the name of the Texan Scotchman was mentioned in the same context as a growing list of conspirators in the assassination. And time and time again a line came back to him: the line of Shakespeare he'd heard the actor speaking at the rehearsal in the Alhambra Theatre. About there being something rotten in the state of Denmark. Well, now he was damn sure there was something rotten in the state of Washington too. And now that the country had been re-unified, the fishermen of Washington cast a wide net . . .

He hadn't been in the capital for very long but in his short stay he'd been close enough to politicians to learn something of their ways; about the constant horse-trading, the behind-back deals, and that truth was a rare commodity amongst the breed. It was clear from what he was reading in the newspapers that someone wanted scapegoats, whether to deflect attention from their own incompetence, or to cover up something more sinister. Lincoln's murder had aroused cries from Northerners for vengeance. He was experienced enough to know, no matter how innocent he was, that he would get a rough deal — or worse — if he returned and declared himself. That is if he could make the return to Washington without some bullet in the dark finding its mark.

His best course of action lay in another direction, to lose himself, let Tom Connor disappear. He deliberately played down his Scottish accent. The way he spoke had been identified in the papers. He let his beard grow and, with the disappearance of a smooth chin, Tom Connor died. He didn't have to think long about a new label. He took his second baptism name and his mother's maiden name of Grimm, and thus Jonathan Grimm, wandering trail-hand, was born.

The man known as Jonathan Grimm saw many things over the next months. On the south-west trail he rode alongside ragged, hungry soldiers returning to homesteads wracked with penury. Great areas of the South had been devastated. The once-proud cities of the Confederacy had had their souls blasted out of them by bombardment and fire. Farming was in stagnation. The Southern currency system had collapsed. The disillusioned turned to crime. And the south was subjected to army rule.

The bad times of the war had given over to the bad days of peace. He thought of returning to Scotland, but after years away he would be as much a stranger in his homeland as here. He spoke differently, he thought differently. So, once more he worked at odd jobs, once more he was restless without purpose.

But the further he travelled, the fewer signs of war did he see. The Confederate Trans-Mississippi Department had remained unconquered throughout the war, maintaining a core of prosperity.

He made it to Indian Territory and fetched up at a ranch with a government contract to supply beef for feeding the

Five Civilized Tribes. It was round-up time and the outfit was short of hands. His wound had healed and he was a capable worker. The boss liked him and, when the season was over, offered him a permanent job as back-up to the ramrod, a solid fellow called Israel.

It was one of the biggest spreads in the territory, the liking was mutual and Tom got on with the other hands in the bunkhouse.

And it gave him the opportunity to bury himself.

* * *

A year passed and he became well-established in the outfit. He knew the routine and was seen as a trusted and hard worker. Come the new spring the warm sun irritated his hairy chin and he cleaned off the beard.

One day he was in the study with the ramrod Israel talking over work schedules with the boss when there was a visitor. That the caller was a senator was no surprise as he had learned that his employer was big in state politics.

"If you'll excuse us, boys," the ranch-owner had said, terminating the session with his workers and indicating for the politician to sit.

The workmen got the point and proceeded to leave.

"Say, your face is familiar," the senator said to the man called Grimm as the two workers clunked their spurred boots towards the door.

Grimm paused and half-turned, avoiding the presentation of a full face. To himself he cursed that he had cleaned away the beard.

"Goddamn, yes," the man went on. "Mighty familiar. You spend much time in Washington, mister?"

"No, sir," Grimm said. "Never been that far east." He forced a chuckle. "Ain't no call for cowpokes in the capital as far as I know."

The other smiled. "Yeah, you're right there. Sure ain't much employment opportunity for beef drovers along

Pennsylvania Avenue." He shook his head. "Nevertheless it's a little strange. Sure seems like I seen you before. But wasn't as a cow handler." He shrugged, dismissed the notion and turned in anticipation to the drink his host was pouring.

During his chores over the next few days Grimm mulled over the incident. The senator had pushed aside the vague recollection, but if they came face to face again, it might prompt the man to reconsider the thought. And with the politicking his employer was prone to, such a meeting was a distinct possibility. He realized that having deliberately laid low for so long would only have made his case worse, should he be recognized and get hauled back to the capital.

Hell, seemed like it was time once again to pull up his picket pin. Mind, wouldn't be too hard. He'd saved over a hundred dollars which he'd lodged in the local bank; enough to grubstake him on the trail again.

He let it set awhile, so that there was no obvious link between his meeting with the senator and his departure, and then made known his decision to leave. His boss laid some store by his employee and tried to persuade him to stay but eventually acknowledged that it was the nature of cowpokes that they came and went.

* * *

A few days on, Grimm made his farewells and rode into town. His work pal Israel had business in town and rode with him. It was early morning and the bank hadn't opened yet. There was a saloon next door so the two men took the opportunity to share a farewell drink while Tom waited. In a bar deserted except for themselves they talked. Eventually the ramrod shook his hand and left to attend to his affairs leaving Grimm to finish his glass.

The Scot himself was just about to leave when he heard shots. He dashed outside and saw two men heavy-footing across the sidewalk coming from the adjacent bank, hefting guns and carrying bulging saddle-bags. Near the hitching rail, a third on horseback held their horses in wait.

A wounded teller was lying in the doorway shouting for help but the main drag was virtually devoid of people. That made Grimm the only person close.

The nearest hardcase saw Grimm and fired, the bullet going wide. Flattening against the wall, Grimm pulled his own gun and returned fire. The first man collapsed while the further one spun round, still gripping the saddle-bag, and triggered his weapon.

Grimm should have taken cover but he had one thought in mind — he had come to town to withdraw his funds and this damn bozo had got his hard-earned money! Lucky for the impetuous Scot the only damage the bank-robber's slug did was to gouge splinters from the jamb of the saloon door. Grimm fired again and caught the man's forearm.

That was enough for the third man who savagely spurred his horse along the main drag, leaving his companions to their fate.

The remaining desperado dropped the saddlebag and clutched at his injured gun arm, trying to raise the weapon.

"It ain't gonna work," Grimm said. "Drop it."

As the man did so, Grimm raised a straightened pistol arm, closed an eye and fired at the receding rider. But the man was well out of range. Grimm turned his attention once more to the still standing man, who was now gripping his arm close to his wound.

As Grimm looked him over, a wave of adrenalin gushed through his body. The man's bandanna mask had fallen — and he recognized the dirty, bristled features that had been revealed. The ugly square face, the wart on the cheek, both were burned into his brain.

Henderson! The man he had sought so long in vain. The man he had given up hope of ever seeing again. Like so many Southerners in post-war times, the bozo had turned to the owlhoot trail. And of all the one-horse towns he had chosen to ride into . . .

The varmint didn't recognize him. Had no call to. They'd only met once and, now in a tight corner, reminiscing was the last thing on the robber's mind.

Grimm advanced. "Henderson," he said slowly. "Henderson, late of the Texas Brigade. Small world."

The man shrugged. "Ain't me, pilgrim."

"The hell it ain't," Grimm grunted. He stepped forward slowly, emotions coming to a focus. "Mary Connor."

"What the hell you on about?"

"No. Figure you don't know. You wouldn't even know her name."

The man was puzzled but didn't like the look in Grimm's eyes or the threatening maw of the advancing gun and began to back along the boardwalk. "Listen, you got me dead to rights knocking over this here bank. Hand me over to the sheriff."

"Mary Connor, you defiled her and killed her."

The man's face blanched.

"That's right," Grimm said, advancing. "It's coming back, ain't it? I'm Tom Connor, her husband." He cleared his throat. "Widower to be technical."

The other regained control but the fear stayed in his eyes. "Don't know what you're talking of, mister."

Grimm ignored the protestation. "Figure at this moment you're feeling somehow like she did. Scared to hell, paining, looking for mercy. You know, scumbag, that makes me feel good. Real good."

"Hey, this is Indian Territory. I ain't even from Texas."

"Neither am I."

Henderson reached the end of the wooden walkway and his expression changed. "Hey, Tom Connor! I *have* heard that name. Yeah. You're wanted too! Wait till I tell folk!"

The man who now called himself Grimm smiled, hard, cynical. "You know what you've just done, pal? Given me a second reason for sending your scumbag soul to hell." And he pulled the trigger.

Henderson rocketed back off the boardwalk and landed in the dust, a crater in his forehead.

Grimm walked to the edge and looked down at the blooded, sunken-eyed death mask. "Not that a second reason was needed."

20

GRIMM was standing in the sheriff's office with the lawman and the bank owner. The sheriff had been out of town during the bank robbery so there had been delay in organizing a posse. It had ridden out along the western trail but the third robber had got too much of a head start and had disappeared into the vastness of the Oklahoman plains.

"Did yourself a fine morning's work, pardner," the lawman was saying, pointing to the Wanted posters on his desk. One showed Henderson's face under a figure of a thousand dollars. "When I've cleared it with the Judicial Department there's a thousand smackeroos coming your way." He flicked a thumb where the remaining thwarted robber was nursing his wound in the cell. "I'm only sorry there ain't nothing for you on that one."

"Anyways, I'll add another five hundred," the bank man said. "For good measure. If more ordinary folk acted like you, the banks wouldn't be so vulnerable. Facing up to three armed hardcases, takes some guts. You have my admiration, Mr Grimm."

"Saved me some paperwork too," the lawman went on, "putting out the varmint's lights the way you did." He paused and looked at the ranch-hand. "Folks tell me he had dropped his gun, but you still shot him."

"The heat of the moment," Grimm said. He'd wondered when someone would raise that. But his answer seemed to satisfy.

"Makes no never mind," the sheriff said. "Reward plainly says dead or alive. You done this kind of thing before?"

"Nope."

"Well, don't feel so bad. There's a first time for everything."

"I don't feel so bad." Grimm looked

beyond the lawman at the Wanted posters on the wall. "There's money on all of those?"

"Sure is."

"You mean a plain citizen can catch a desperado and take him in for rewards?"

"To the nearest law office. That's the way it's done. There's a small number of guys live by bounty-hunting." The lawman studied the other man's face, the epitomy of seriousness. "You looking for a gainful occupation, Mr Grimm?"

There had been years in his life when he had lived without purpose. Then for a long spell he had lived for one thing: to find Henderson. Now he had despatched the critter to Hades, what next? He had nothing to live for. He had no itch to settle anymore. All that hard work that could be blown away in an instant. Moreover, he had been the kiss of death to two women and had no desire to jeopardize a third. Now, bounty-hunting, that was a possibility. "Gainful occupation," he echoed. "Could be."

"A warning for free, Mr Grimm. Ain't an easy trail. They're all hard men. Plant a man who's dogging 'em as soon as look at him."

Grimm picked up the remaining poster with a picture of the escaped horseman. Frank Frean. There was four hundred on him. Less than he'd already earned from the present episode, but if he was going to try his hand at this bounty-hunting caper he had to start somewhere.

"I was aiming to leave town when I got caught up in this shindig," Grimm said. "And, if I'm gonna light out after this Frean, I really wanna get my legs forked. How long will it take to settle up with the money?"

"Now we've got the telegraph in town should clear it by tomorrow."

"And I can pay you five hundred cash in the time that it takes to walk back to my office," the bank man said.

"Then in that case I'll check in at

the hotel," Grimm said. "Give myself time to rest up and make preparations. This bozo's trail will be cold by now so I don't have to head out immediately. But I don't want to delay getting after him for too long."

"Understandable," the lawman said, taking his hand. "And the best of luck, Mr Grimm."

★ ★ ★

Jonathan Grimm, prospective bounty-hunter, set out the next day heading west. There was over one and a half grand in his saddle-bags and a folded dodger on Frank Frean in his jacket pocket.

Once more he had confidence and a purpose in life. He had learned things about himself. He could track a man. He'd already demonstrated that skill with John Wilkes Booth — and he'd beaten the country's military in getting to the man, to boot. That sure as hell proved something.

More, he could handle his side guns. He'd never given conscious thought to that, but soldiering in the war between the states had honed his expertise in weapon handling.

The job required riding hard trails and rough country, and that meant horses — and he sure knew his horses.

Each of these was an essential quality in a man who chose to try his hand at bringing owlhoots to justice. But more important, the previous day he'd learned something else about himself. Something that would give him the edge in his new calling.

Like the sheriff had said, he had faced three armed men, hardcases with no compunction against killing. What he hadn't told the sheriff was that he had felt no fear. That fact hadn't registered with him till after the event — but the eventual realization of it had made him think. Why had he not been a-feared of dying when he faced three guns? He was an ordinary guy, wasn't he?

Maybe. But maybe he had died already: twice in fact, when his cherished women had met their violent ends. Whatever the reason, he knew now he felt no fear of the long sleep: that was an ace in the hole for a man choosing to lead a violent life in a violent country.

The sheriff had told him the trade was despised. So what? He could handle that: he already knew what it meant to be reviled.

He had another item in his pocket: a print-damp copy of the town newspaper. He'd read it once, shook his head in near disbelief and tucked it away. Told a story in fanciful terms, how a bank-robber called Henderson had met the Grim Reaper in the shape of a fearless public-spirited citizen by the name of Jonathan Grimm. The editor had wanted Grimm to pose for a photograph but he had balked. Understandable, the newsman had said, might attract vengeance of some sort. Grimm kept his real reason for not wanting his features publicized to himself. So the paper had made do with a rough portrait sketch that, happily, bore little resemblance to the features of the erstwhile Scot. It was the line underlying the caption that had made him shake his head with a cold smile: The Reaper Grimm.

* * *

And how he was to fare under his new label has been recorded in *Guns of the Reaper* and other chronicles listed at the beginning of the present book.

THE END